I0782081

PHASE

PHASE

James West

ISBN: 978-1-961017-73-3 (sc)
ISBN: 978-1-961017-74-0 (e)

Rev. date: 07/17/2023

CONTENTS

CHAPTER ONE

My name is Alison Riley, and you're looking at me, with my bluejeans and my tank top, sitting here on my living room couch on a Sunday afternoon, and you're thinking what's this girl doing wasting her time talking to me when she ought to be outside, breaking some hearts, ha ha, you just know that's what I like to do, right? You've been checking out my apartment, yeah, it's pretty nice, yeah, I bought all the furniture myself, and yeah, it's all mine and I live here by myself. So you know I do pretty well for a twenty-five year old girl. And yeah, I've been around, I guess you could say I've broken my share of hearts. What girl hasn't? You can't help it these days, my God, they're all out there just begging for it. I'm sure if I walked outside wearing this tank top I wouldn't get two blocks without getting asked out. That's just the way it is out there, I'm used to it, you know, in fact it's a lot of fun to be a girl and know a lot of guys are looking at you. I guess I can't help but feel a little spoiled. I don't think it's anything serious though, you know, I don't think I've got a swelled head over it. Getting along with guys just isn't the major preoccupation of my life, you see, and maybe that's because I've never had to try hard to get them to like me. Sometimes they're hanging over me so much that it's all I can do to get away from them. And the thing is, I like guys too, I like them a lot, but most of them are so bloody obsessed with being the most depraved idiot possible and they think this is supposed to turn girls on or something. Sometimes they really make me ill.

I'm not feeling very good now, in fact, and it's because of some guys I know. These guys I really know well. Because of these guys I'll never be quite the way I used to be ever again. I guess you might say they brought me in touch with myself. Well, nowadays being in touch with myself is an experience that just makes me want to cry my guts out. So I've learned to…to kind of…stay out of touch with… with that. I'm functioning the same as ever, I still go to work, I get around—but the real me—I know that's just some ball of pain that I can't face. I just can't face that too much.

Okay, I'm sorry, this isn't the way I wanted to start it all out. The thing is, behind all the words I can talk to you with, the truth of my life is…is this ball of pain, and it occurred to me a little while back that that's the real reason I'm telling you all this. I mean, I really think it's this is kind of a beautiful story, you know, and a lot of it is so great, and funny, and you're going to laugh at a lot of it. A lot of it you're probably going to think, this has got to be the stupidest stuff I've ever heard. And a lot of it you'll probably think should never have happened, or wouldn't have happened if a certain people hadn't been out of their minds, or maybe if a few certain people had thought differently—used a little understanding instead of doing what they did.

That's why, more than anything else I feel about all this, now that it's happened, it's over, and now—now, there's nothing I can do—nothing anybody can do to—make it—the way it—just any way but the way it is now—that's why I've just got to tell you the real story, the whole crazy story, from my side, 'cause I was there right from the beginning, and nobody knows what really happened better than I do. Anybody can read a newspaper. I read the newspapers, I saw the news on TV. You saw a bunch of lawyers and reporters and some lady reading some script they handed her and it was all so bloody predictable and about as meaningful as washing the dishes. Well, for them and you I guess they may be as meaningful as it will ever be.

Aw, now I'm starting to get sarcastic, that's just what I'm trying to avoid. I've always been sarcastic about things, and usually because that's the only way to cope with a lot of situations that stink so bad you just kind of hold your nose and pretend they smell like roses. Right now…right now, if you want to know the truth, if I were to let myself go and really communicate what I'm feeling, look, I'd be bawling my eyes out, man, I'd be just making a damned fool of myself. So I've gotta get a little sarcastic just so I can start to make sense.

So now I guess you're starting to get the picture of me in your head of this chick who thinks she pretty much knows herself, maybe a little too well, knows what she can do, but just does what she wants, huh? Well, that's just about right. Yeah, I could be all dressed up for a night of swinging adventure downtown, spending my time obliging all those insatiable males and their dreams of glory. What the hell, I know I'll be back on the barroom scene any day now, living it up and loving every minute of it, yeah, I know myself well enough to know that as soon as I get all this stuff off my chest I'll be like a brand new Alison Riley again.

For now, though, I just want to stay here at home with you, real quiet and peaceful, where nobody and nothing can interrupt us, while I get this out of my system.

Okay. The first thing you've got to know about me is that what you see here, this chick who's sitting here at home in her jeans spilling her every emotion and personal opinion like some maladjusted hippie at an encounter session, well, I'm sure this is giving you precisely the most opposite perception of the real me that's possible in a five-minute first impression. So let me set you straight right now, Alison Riley is firstly and lastly a survivor. Whatever else I might end up doing, however bent and obsessed and freaking full of myself I might get over men or work or Chinese Food for crying out loud, and as much as I may despise it, AND I do; taking care of business, man, that's ninety-nine percent of my life, that's what I do and I get it done good. Monday through Friday, nine to five, that's how it's been for the past four years and seeing as how I've managed to double my salary in that time working at the same company, well, I feel real good about that, and all the stupid petty office politics and image bartering and compromising I've had to do, and still have to do, hey, like, strangely enough I've even learned to enjoy it. It all means paycheck to me, furniture and clothes and food and my own apartment. I think I'm lucky to have a little seniority where I work now, and I like the feeling that I know what I'm going to be doing eight hours a day, five days a week. In fact, it's the ability to enjoy times like this, man, that's what makes me love what I do, how I make my living. To say it could be worse would be the understatement of the decade.

By the way, what I do from dawn to twilight five days a week is called being an administrative assistant to a corporate lawyer in a Washington D. C. law firm. He usually refers to me as his secretary.

It's really hard work. When I was starting out, after I'd just graduated with a liberal arts bachelor's degree from a little known college in southwestern Virginia, and I was first facing the prospect of C. R. T.'s and copiers and collating and telephones and legal terms of which I hadn't the faintest comprehension and then, worst of all, Dear Lord in Heaven, the PAPER—letterheads and second sheets and writs and torts and injunctions and litigations and all on all these papers to be numbered and collated and mailed and printed and sorted and shredded…when I was first starting out I remember rehearsing for my resignation speech at least ten times a day, alternating of course with summoning up every last vestige of what remained of my common sense, or instinct for self-preservation, and hammering down the burgeoning nausea with something like, "you don't work, Alison, you don't eat."

I hated it.

But after about year of this I came to the realization that I was actually performing a level of work that nobody short of an Einsteinian prodigy could hope to duplicate. That's when I got my first big raise too. All of a sudden I took so much pride in myself that it seemed they couldn't pile enough paper on my desk. I started attacking assignments like I was training for the heavyweight championship of the world. The harder the work got, the more I liked it, and it's been that way for the last three years.

Now, you're thinking, wait a minute. Just a few minutes ago I was saying how I despised what I called "taking care of business". Well, that's still true. But you'll remember I said that taking care of business was ninety-nine percent of my life. That other one percent—that's the infinitesimal piece that I allow myself for every feeling and emotion and moments that I call precious and especially—since I've learned how to organize everything so well—my ideas.

My ideas—nothing could be further from the other ninety-nine percent of the iceberg of my life.

The things I like to think about, that start my heart pounding…I never know when or where, all of a sudden, I'll get some fantastic feeling of joy or pride or happiness or ridiculousness, Christ, I don't know how to describe it…it's like some joke that's been sitting in the back of my mind had just for the first time seemed funny, really hilariously funny, instead of, you know, "so funny I forgot to laugh." If it's a really, really good idea, I start getting even more ideas, and by the time I'm on my sixth or even seventh idea, Oh God, I'm hiding in the lady's room, doubled up over the toilet, laughing and crying so uncontrollably I'm afraid I'd be committed if anyone found me. Luckily, I don't get ideas that good very often.

What do I mean by ideas like this? Here's one I had just the other day. It was around lunchtime, and my boss had sent me to the store to pick up some cleaning supplies. There I was, standing in line with about thirty dollars worth of paper towels and scouring powder, ant spray and wastepaper basket liners, and unavoidably, the unappetizing combination of resenting this mundane task of doing my boss's shopping and loathing the near certainty that it would fall to me to implement these thirty dollars' worth of cleaning materials; standing in line, anonymously waiting in the midst of perhaps a hundred other shoppers, with all my feelings of working somehow beyond the strictures of my job description nonwithstanding; it was then that this notion came, this crystal-clear vision of my boss's face, twisting into an expression of complete consternation as a cassette tape that I had sent him in the mail disgorges howl after howl of nothing but the most depraved laughter I could record while splashing around in my bathtub. Well, that wasn't one of my best ideas, but it was good enough that I had to lean on the candy rack and clamp my hand on my mouth to keep from completely spasming out in the middle of line.

Here's a better one, I think. I went to the movie theatre recently to see a matinee showing of Bambi. You know how these shows are, hundreds of kids between five and ten years of age screaming "Thumper!" and "Flower!" whenever these characters first appear on the screen. All the time I was watching the movie, I thought of standing up in the middle of one of these ovations and bellowing "SHUT UP!!" at the top of my lungs. I was chortling over that one all the way until Bambi's mother got shot.

That's what most of my ideas are like, completely absurd and utterly opposite to the way I run my life and the way others see me. As you might guess, my ideas get downright dangerous sometimes. Oh yes, and even anti-social. That's why I absolutely, positively, resolutely refuse to ever actually tell anybody my ideas, that is to say, in so many spoken words. Oh, no, if there's one thing I've learned working in a corporate legal environment, it's the necessity to maintain that dedicated and loyal image. But most importantly, I had found another way to express my wild and bizarre ideas, a way that not only was safe for sensitive egos but also lots of fun and a great way to meet guys too. About two years ago, one night as I was walking home from the Metrorail station, thinking as usual about how nice it would soon be in my quiet little bathtub, a wonderful inspiration seemed to dawn on me, like so many other of my ideas that never saw fruition. Maybe it had come from riding in the high- tech sterility of the Metro train, the energy and the rhythm of the cars; whatever it was, that night, as I laid back on my bathtub, I scanned up and down through the classified section of the Washington Post, looking for a good deal on…a drum set.

Sure enough, there was one for sale for less than two hundred dollars. I think I was still dripping wet from my bath when I called up 'Kevin' and arranged to come over to his house to look at the set, an old Ludwig five-piece. And I'm sure I would have bought it even if it wasn't finished in such a beautiful glittering blue, or if Kevin hadn't offered to transport it to my apartment. I'm sure I would have bought it, because I had decided that night that drumming was the only socially acceptable way to express all my crazy, neurotic, obsessed feelings.

Of course, I didn't become a legend in the annals of percussion overnight. I just set up the kit in a corner of my apartment, and every once in a while I'd turn on my favorite rock and roll radio station, turn up the volume pretty high, and just kind of groove along to whatever songs they'd play; basically just trying to duplicate exactly whatever drumming I was hearing on the stereo. It really wasn't that hard. In fact, after about a week of spending maybe an hour a night at this, I was starting to really get into it. I was actually turning down dates with guys because now I looked forward to learning drum rolls, polishing my bass pedal technique, or just sitting back and admiring my glittering blue drum kit.

I never told anyone about my new hobby. Keeping it a secret seemed almost necessary in order to translate wanton, forbidden ideas into drumming. As the weeks went by, and I grew more and more accustomed to the feel of the wooden drumsticks and the leather drumheads, I found myself developing a strangely joyful confidence, where before, if anything, there had been only a kind of shameful, alienated guilt for harboring that unspeakable one-percent of my personality. Drumming to the rock and roll songs that played on my living-room stereo was becoming the perfect way to reconcile the differences between my business-like self and the part of me that needed to rebel, refute, and reject the hypocrisy and fascism that I saw in the world I depended on for my livelihood. As overly idealized as that my sound, that's exactly what my drums were able to do for me; the exertion of pounding them released so much aggression that after thirty minutes or so I'd feel more peaceful and relaxed than after having sex with any guy that comes to mind. And in addition to that, I could feel myself getting better and better every night, until, after a couple of months, I felt so 'at one' with my Ludwigs that I was bashing out my own off-beats and flams on top of the radio drum beats. In other words, I was starting to get kind of proud of myself, and that felt pretty good.

Even more profound than these reasons, though, was the almost indescribable thrill I felt, when a really driving, power-chord laden, utter energy-bombard of a rock song would come on the stereo, and I could fuse the bursting, blasting cracks of my snare into a meshing, braided pattern of tom-toms and bass, riding on my cymbals for a velvety-crisp lead break, then slamming back into a minimalist back beat finale; that "slamming" moment, that's it, that's the best, that's the point of satori in the 'zen' of my ideas, and oh, God, when I first started getting it down right, it was all I could do to keep myself from falling off of the drum throne, oh, the magical release of it all, the feeling of power, if anything in the world is as good or better than sex it's this.

Well, enough of that. Like I started to say before, the best thing about drumming was the way that, instead of interfering with the business part of my life, it really started to improve it. The whole idea of having this secret drum set, and this ever-increasing ability to play it, would, more and more often, come to me at some random point in the middle of my workday, perhaps when I'd be feeling frustrated over a pile of paperwork that wouldn't go away, or triggered by some piece of particularly small-minded office rhetoric, and I would think of how my irritation would become translated into a raging tom-tom barrage climaxed by a snare roll into a shimmering fountain of cymbals; and a smile would traipse across my face, and like so much trivial, rippling waters, my work troubles would seem almost to be soothing the restless soul of my unknowable one-percent.

Hee hee hee…I love my glittering blue drum set.

CHAPTER TWO

The offices that I work at are located just about in the center of Washington, D. C., on the tenth floor of this building; it's really a terrific place to work. To give you an idea of how opulent this place is, I found out one time that the rent our company is charged for that one floor of office space is close to two million dollars per year. The minute you walk into the first floor lobby from the street, the impression you might get is that you've entered the Hanging Gardens of Babylon, at least that's how I always think of it. All around you, walls of shining, green, veined marble ascend to the uppermost heights of the fifteen story building from a floor that is also a parquet of green and white marble. The decor is a mixture of hundreds of potted ivy plants either hanging from above on brass chains or set on the floor in corners by the elevator entrances or the other doors. Coming off of the dirty, noisy hostility of the Washington street into this sanctuary, where all one can perceive is the babble of the hundreds of serious conversations and the billion dollar panorama of cool green stone, is one amazingly impressive transition. Though I've done it a thousand times, it seems to me the gratitude and respect I feel for being able to work in the midst of such a sanctuary is increasing all the time.

Every Monday through Friday I'll get on board one of the brass-doored elevators that takes me to the law offices. There, the walls are more conventional sheet rock, painted white and accessoried with occasional wall sconces, the floor covered wall-to-wall with grey indoor-outdoor carpeting. The halls of our offices are always brightly lit with the whitest of fluorescent overhead fixtures. I'll pass by the receptionist desk and turn a couple of corners to get to my desk, a secretarial station raised a couple of inches from the corridor level by a pedestal.

This pedestal effect was no doubt devised by some architect to convey the idea of our importance to the firm's clients. There are close to thirty secretarial stations on our floor, each of which have two secretaries sitting next to each other at two desks. This design, again, no doubt was arrived at with the idea that no secretary would have so much privacy that she would mix too much personal business with her work; there would always be someone close at hand to keep her in check. In my case, I'd been sitting at the same desk, working for the same lawyer, for all of the last four years. Sitting in the cubicle next to me had always been a secretary who would seem to last almost exactly one year before she would move on to another job.

As I mentioned before, by the time I'd been working at the firm for a couple of years I had reached the level at which I could know pretty much exactly what to expect to be doing every day. I'd arrive at my desk a little early every morning, water my plants, put a newspaper into my boss's office, little things like that; until nine o'clock came by, and my neighboring secretary would show up, along with my boss, and all the other secretaries and their bosses; and telephones would start ringing and typewriters would start chattering and people would start running up and down the halls. For my part, I would immerse myself in my responsibilities, and because this always meant copying and taking dictation and transcribing and generally making sure that my boss's work got onto paper and onto the street, as long as I would do exactly as I was told and never let my personal thoughts of feeling intrude, everything went smoothly, five o'clock would eventually come and I would go home with a light conscience. And, like I said before, as far as personal feelings and thoughts were concerned, there were ninety-nine times as much business aspects of me to outweigh them.

Which isn't to say that I was an unsocial animal at work, oh no, far from it. As time went by, and I dealt with generally the same people day after day, the intensity of my business-oriented attitude and performance made me more popular than I could have hoped to become if I had concentrated, instead, on wearing the most provocative blouses or spent a lot of time joining in the office gossip or noticing any of the men who worked there. I made a conscious effort to stick to conservative clothing, and when I might hear somebody's name being made a topic of less-than-business type speculation, I would employ what I'd earnestly developed within myself to either change the subject or think of somewhere else I could be. Not surprisingly, at least to me, by avoiding all the more petty affairs that so fascinate people, who really ought to have something better to do, and instead concentrating on getting work and only work done, I succeeded in building an image of pure reliability; this was a success that I enjoyed sharing with my boss and co-workers…

Now, about one hundred and fifty people work down at our firm, and this number is roughly composed of about sixty secretaries, working for about sixty professionals, which leaves a remainder of about thirty, of which about ten are high-level executives like the chairman of the board, the president and the vice-presidents, and finally some fifteen-to-twenty support staffers, like a few mail clerks, maintenance, and the office services people, which included a few receptionists, assistants, and other people with their own particular jobs. Though I work "entirely" for my boss, Mr. Carruthers, I have interaction with almost everybody down there at one time or another, whether it's with the support staffers who provide us with pens and paper, or the maintenance people who take out our trash and vacuum the floor, or all the other secretaries, who either need to borrow my white-out, or need change for the Coke machine, or, if I let them, would burden me with the epic tales of how their husbands are failing them.

There was one individual with whom I'd interact every day, the office services clerk, George Kerns. It was upon George that all the secretaries and professionals would rely for everything from their morning coffees to their letterhead stationery. George worked out of a small supply room located down the hall from us, where a stockpile of every office supply used at the firm was maintained. Whenever we would need copy paper or pens or white-out or paper clips, we would fill out a standardized pink requisition form and bring it to the supply room, and George would pile the supplies on the shelf of his little window for us to take back to our desks. In addition to this, he would maintain our coffee rooms with coffee, styrofoam cups, sugar, creamer, and tea. He had a few other duties, such as helping move people's furniture when they changed offices, and no doubt there was much he did that I wasn't aware of. Unlike any other employee of our firm,

George was rather unique, in that he functioned sort of as everybody's assistant, kind of like all the secretaries' secretary.

George started working at the firm about two and a half years after I did. I remember the day we were introduced, his first day at work. Derrie Grant, the office services manager, was walking him around on a tour of the firm's various areas, and I was sitting at my desk, entering some documents into my word processor.

"Alison," Derrie called out in her particular version of the concisely cheerful office manner, "I'd like you to meet George Kerns. He is going to be our new office services clerk."

Since it was our first meeting, I smiled perfunctorily, stood, and extended my hand down to the shyly smiling, black-haired man. If anything, I was thinking he looked uncomfortable in his shirt and tie, which somehow seemed the wrong attire for the rather peculiar- looking person squinting back at me. But more likely I was so preoccupied with the work I was doing that I took little interest in the formality of introducing a new employee. George nodded and said, "Pleased to meet you." and Derrie, naturally wanting to get her orientation duties over as quickly as possible, explained how I was Mr. Carruther's secretary, embellishing it with a few complimentary remarks about how long and how reliably I'd been working for the firm; and after giving us an opportunity to make some small talk,

ushered him on down the hall. Deeply entrenched in my work at the time, I didn't give our meeting any more consideration.

In the days that followed, though, I would see George more than anybody in the firm with the exception of my boss, as the skinny, distracted-looking new employee undertook his position and soon could be seen shuttling back and forth the halls of the firm, usually carrying boxes of stationery or pens, struggling to keep up with the demands of all the secretaries and lawyers. I gradually became familiar with his particular approach and professional personality; and saw that, like myself, George was extremely focused on the job at hand, and went out of his way to satisfy the sometimes eccentric requirements that came his way. Even if we didn't become more than somewhat passing acquaintances, it was pleasant to see him going about his work, cheerily saying "Hi" and "How ya doin'?" virtually every time we'd meet, and soon I felt I could rely on him to be punctual and competent, as others relied on myself. That was the image of George that remained in my mind; but perhaps even more than anyone else who worked at the firm, he never really registered with me on a personal level. It wasn't until about six months after he'd been working there that I realized this.

That's the point, about a year ago, when everything started to change. Speaking from the hindsight I've gained since then, I can start to describe for you the unusual case of George.

The reason that neither I nor anybody took much notice of him was that, beyond being helpful as courteous as he was, there didn't seem to be much to George that anybody could be interested in. He wasn't particularly attractive, he certainly wasn't repulsively overweight, and the way he behaved and the work he did was, like I said, exemplary. He always wore a shirt and tie and kept well-groomed, and even smelled good, unlike lots of other people that come to mind.

The fact of the matter, though, is that George really came off best when he was doing something for somebody, and he had a kind of atmosphere about him that spoke of loneliness, desperation for something to do, impatience—it was as if, were he not immersed in doing something for you, he wouldn't know what to do with himself. At least repulsively overweight people have some kind of personality that at least can make people feel empathy for them; George, well, he just seemed to have some kind of non-existent core. You could talk to him, even try to share some of your inner feelings with him, and he'd just kind of smile distantly, maybe nod, and then either you'd find some kind of excuse to leave, or he would. Sometimes all he'd have to say was this almost retarded, drawn-out and vague "Uhhhh…". Cold as it may sound, there was a disturbing kind of menace that seemed to lurk behind his eyes, making people want to avoid him; out of respect for his high level of job performance, I always tried to be friendly with him, but even I felt put off by that strange, somehow inhuman quality of his, and like everyone else I ignored him to a great extent…that is, until about a year ago.

As if it were a yearly tradition, the position of the secretary next to me had become vacant again. Passing by on his daily rounds, George had taken notice of the empty desk and was making a habit of asking when the "mystery secretary" was going to arrive. She appeared around the beginning of last October. Along came Derrie Grant that Monday morning with a girl whose beaming, enthusiastic smile dazzled me immediately.

"Alison, I'd like you to meet the girl who will be working next to you. Joan, this is Alison Riley, who's been working here—what, two years?"

"Three." I rose to shake the new girl's hand. "Pleased to meet you… Miss—Joan…?"

"Stevens." chirped the girl in one of the most strikingly cheerful voices I'd ever heard, so different from the dolorous tones usually heard at the firm. Her big brown eyes were heavily accented by blue eyeshadow, but in her case somehow the effect was not overdone. "I'm pleased to meet you, Alison!" She shook my hand and laughed when I returned her smile, impressing me that this was one mischievous and perhaps immature person. Her hair was shortly cropped, it may have been blonde but it shone with an almost orange hue, and her slender figure was outfitted in a dark blue dress that would have served her splendidly on a date with any of the guys I knew.

"Joan, this is going to be your workstation. You'll enjoy working next to Alison, I'm sure. This is your C. R. T., and your boss, Mr. Gibbs', office is directly across." Derrie was in her usual hurry. "So, why don't I just leave you here with Alison and let you two get to know each other?"

"This is such a beautiful office!" Joan practically sang as she sat down at her desk. "It's hard to believe we're right in the middle of D. C., you know what I mean?"

"Uh huh." I replied casually. "Are you very familiar with our computer system?"

"Oh, yes, it's no problem. I've been studying Computer Architecture. This system will be a breeze."

"Computer Architecture, huh?" I was pretty impressed.

"Yes. I don't want to be a secretary all of my life." Joan huffed with a cock of her head.

"Really? What kind of career did you have in mind?"

"Well, I'm not sure right now. There's so much that a career in computer programming can open up for you…but I know one thing, and that's that I want to make a lot more money than I'm making now!" She was still smiling that amazing smile.

"Good for you." I replied as sincerely as possible. "If there's anything I can help you with, let me know."

"Thanks, Alison." she giggled. I started to busy myself with my work, but the impression I was getting from my new neighbor was so intriguing that I wanted very much to continue finding out more about her. Though my ninety-nine percent business personality couldn't rationally explain it, my secret and intuitive one percent was sensing that there was a lot going on for this girl; as if somehow the sum of her parts exceeded her whole; I sensed a powerfully disconcerting magnetism about her, a dynamism that would have been profound even if she weren't so undeniably beautiful, but gorgeous as she was, the effect was downright fascinating. Of all the girls who had occupied the seat next to mine, none had this girl's intensity of brash, self-confident ambition, combined with such obvious intelligence and such a rare, stunning beauty, that even I as a woman could not help admiring. What kind of reaction would this produce in the men of the office? It was against my better nature, that is, my normal impartiality, but I felt my hidden one percent groaning in curiosity, forcing me to look at her left hand to see if she wore a ring. There were many.

"Are you married, Joan?" I asked.

"Oh, no, not yet." she replied, as if it were an achievement to be proud of. "I'm having too much fun! Why would anybody want to get married?"

"Hunhh!" I grunted ironically. "Good question."

"I'll say." She was busying herself in setting up her dictionary, stationery and writing implements. "I'm doing very well on my own right now, and I like it that way. But I do have a few boyfriends."

"A few?" It bothered me that I took such interest in someone's social life. Would I want someone as interested in mine?

"Sure!" Joan responded, as if it were the most natural thing in the world. "How about you?"

:"Well, I'm not seeing anyone very seriously right now." I thought of my drum set and how my rather private hobby had overridden my social drives.

"Well, Alison," Joan leaned over, her eyebrows lifting and her voice lowering to a conspiratorial whisper. "Just between you and me, I don't take any of my guys very seriously either. In fact, if you really want my opinion, I think all men are a bunch of sluts!"

I stared at her, nodded and smiled, and returned, as best as my distracted state of mind would allow, to my work. The blatant anomaly of my new neighbor continued to disturb me, and her last statement especially piqued my sensibilities. If men were sluts, I wondered, what did that make women? And more pointedly, Ms. Joan Stevens, what did that make you?

CHAPTER THREE

Once Joan Stevens had begun working next to me, things started happening pretty quickly. How long does it take the average man to react to a girl who looks like she stepped out of a centerfold? That's about how long it took for the workstation next to mine to become the hub of more non-legal activity minute for minute than I'd seen in all the days I'd worked there. Flowers clustered on Joan's desk as if she were a subsidiary of FTD, and a day wouldn't pass when at least five men, most probably regretting that they were married, would have interrupted us in our work to remark upon how industrious we were and remind us that all work and no play would make us dull girls. All the while, Joan would oblige them with her deliriously teasing laughter, or promise that if she weren't so behind in her work that she'd love to play with them all day. With all the hanky-panky that seemed virtually crawling out of the woodwork to vie for Joan's attentions, it's a testimony to her exceptional intelligence that she was able to get her work done, and excellently, at that. For my own part, I had to make an extra effort to maintain concentration on my own job, while next to me Joan either held court with the insatiable legions of her fan club or put on a performance of secretarial acumen that quite honestly made the rest of us seem dull and uninspired.

I know for a fact that if Joan had been paired off with any other secretary in the company, there would have been at least twenty-five percent more malicious and time-wasting gossip at the firm's coffee-rooms, water coolers and lunches than there already was. In that respect, Joan was fortunate to have me, the ninety-nine percenter, as a workstation mate; occasionally I'd get jealous of her, and occasionally I'd be amused at the lengths men would go to impress her, but too much of me is a serious businesswoman for me to fail to appreciate the brilliant talent this woman combined with all the rest of her carefree behavior. In the final analysis, much as I might resent the way the effects of her charms made my work difficult, I was in awe of her. Feeling that her professional reputation would benefit most if less were heard, I spoke to no one about her; I knew that at the rate things were going, she'd have more attention than she wanted soon without my help.

What I hadn't foreseen was from whom that attention would come. He came, pushing a hand-truck loaded with copier paper, perspiration glistening beneath the black hair that matted his serious features, the face with those strangely disturbing eyes. He stopped at our workstation that morning, wiped his brow, and smiled at Joan, who had been telling me about her Computer Architecture classes.

"Gee, Alison, is this the mystery secretary? Aren't you going to introduce me?"

"Ha ha ha!" I laughed. "Yes, George, this is the mystery secretary. Joan Stevens, this is George Kerns, the office services assistant. He's the guy who gets you all your supplies and stuff."

"Yeah. Need some copy paper?" George waved a hand at the hand-truck loaded with hundreds of pounds of the stuff. "This could be your last chance, get it while it's blank!"

Joan laughed. I was pleased to see poor, lonely old George making a positive impression on her. "Oh, I've got all I can use right now, kind sir, but I'll be sure to come to you when I need more!"

"And I will be honored to oblige," George declared grandly with a dramatic bow, "Nice to meet you." With that he started pushing his heavy load down the hall. We could hear him muttering, "So…the mystery secretary arrives at last—" as he disappeared from view.

"Isn't he cute?" Joan chattered as she started up her word processor.

"Yes, that's George all right. He's a pretty funny guy." He had been funny for a change, but to myself I was thinking how he was funny, as in peculiar. I also was reacting to how overt George had been,

with the grandiloquent bowing and all that "mystery secretary" business. Even though George had always been cheerful and cooperative with me, these little bits of show-biz were definitely excessive. I sighed inwardly, thinking about how Joan had just won herself another fan.

The next time George came by, not much later on in the week, he stopped and made a big deal of noticing the vase of flowers on Joan's desk, sniffing them with such an exaggerated expression of bliss on his face that both Joan and I broke up laughing.

"Ah, a rose by any other name..." he murmured rapturously... "would...," and then he lapsed into his idiosyncratic, "Uhhhh...".

"You silly!" Joan blurted out. "Those are daffodils!"

"Well, I'm sure daffodils by any other name would...uhhhh...". His myopic-looking eyes rolled toward his forehead.

I thought Joan was going to laugh herself into a spasm. George was obviously beside himself with his own introverted brand of joy. The whole sappy scene was making me nauseous. It took a great deal of effort to continue with the file I was entering into my computer. George hung around for about five minutes, making small talk with Joan, who seemed happy to accomodate him. I thought it was very unusual that George would take the time to socialize with someone at work, and knowing Joan as I did, I began to smell trouble. When George finally left, she was giggling and smiling her most mischievous smile.

"I think George has a crush on me!" "Oh, really?" I replied noncommittally.

"Yes! Did you see the way he was blushing right now?" "No, I must have missed it."

"We were talking about what kinds of music we liked to listen to, and I told him that I like to sing, and he says that he likes to write music."

"Um hmm." I was still forcing myself to concentrate on my document-entering.

"Well," Joan continued, her voice rising with merriment, "When I told him I thought it would be fun to perform with him, he turned the deepest red you ever saw!" At this, she broke into a peal of self- amused laughter.

"Joan, do you really think you ought to be getting so involved with George?"

"What's that supposed to mean?" she asked, her laughter suddenly gone, but with a smile of coy incomprehension remaining on her face. "We were only talking a little bit."

"Yes, but George…" I started to say, but thought better of it, remembering my policy of non-involvement with matters like the one I feared could develop with these two; but something had to be said, I realized, as Joan, still fixing that pseudo-innocent gaze upon me, waited for me to make my point. "George is a real nice guy, Joan, but he's not liable to take things like they're all just a little joke, like you do."

"Oh, Ali." Joan pouted, using the nickname she had devised for me. "You don't think he's—you know—like he'd actually take me seriously, do you?"

"Look, Joan, I've been working here for four years, and I've seen what can happen when people start mixing business with pleasure. Thank goodness, I've never gotten involved with it, and I don't want to get involved now. But to answer your question—I think George is probably the loneliest guy who works at the firm, and I've seen him bust his ass just trying to gain approval from people. That's why I think it wouldn't take much encouragement from you to make him…"

"Yes? Make him what?" Joan's air of feigned naivete' was gaining an edge of indignation. I know I shouldn't have gotten involved, I told myself; I never get involved with these things. Why am I doing this?

"To make him—fall for you."

"Oh, that's silly!" Joan spouted. "George? He's the office services assistant!"

"So?" I asked, although, by the manner of her statement, I could anticipate her next answer.

"Well, you know what I mean. I mean, you don't think that George would think that I would be interested in—oh, come on, it would be like having hamburger instead of—like, steak, you know?"

Yes, I know, Joan, it's not like fascism hasn't come up and spat in my face before.

"I mean, I'm awfully sorry, but even George couldn't be thinking something like that." she pronounced, swiveling her chair to return to work. "He's a funny guy. I like funny guys."

"Well, I hope you're right."

"You know," Joan was giggling again. "There was a client of my boss who I was talking to the other day, and I could tell he really wanted to, uh, have some fun, right? And this guy just happened to slip into the conversation that he's making more than a hundred thousand dollars a year! Ha! I mean, seriously, Ali, how interested is that going to make me with a—a guy that pushes a hand-truck full of copy paper?".

"I see your point," I replied, thinking she could hide it if she brushed her hair differently. "But do you think George would?"

"For heaven's sake, Ali, if I had to worry about hurting the feelings of every man who wanted to get into my pants I really don't think I'd have any time left for work!" Now the tone of Joan's voice had become patronizing and self-righteous. "I mean, what's the big deal over George anyway, I think I've talked to him, what, twice now? For all I know, it sounds to me like maybe you're jealous or something!" She laughed her laugh again, shaking her head, and as if nothing had ever happened, her fingers were flying over her keyboard, her face a mask of concentration on her work.

I think at that point a minor war was raging between my ninety-nine and my one percent. I had never wanted to get involved with anything like this, it went against every part of me that had disciplined itself so stringently to shut out the trivial and concentrate on the important. Yet, I could just feel my one percent reacting, deep inside of me, my emotional ideas screaming at me to strike back at this self-serving wenchlike teasemonger. Ninety-nine percent of me just didn't need all this.

Meanwhile, that same ninety-nine percent was coldly and rationally assessing the situation and was coming to the conclusion that, in her own ludicrous and flighty way, Joan had been almost right about one thing; but it wasn't jealousy I felt, rather than a powerful instinct to defend poor George, with his simple, unsuspecting nature, from the ruthlessly calculating vixen that lurked behind those batting blue eyelids. For the first time in my four years as a career woman, I decided that, if things progressed as they were threatening to, I might have no ethical choice than to intervene, no matter how it might conflict with my interests, in some personal way, to ensure that someone's innocent feelings weren't crushed by someone's insensitive idea of a joke.

In the days that followed, my work continued to inundate me as usual, and after making the decision to take sides with George I found my conscience sufficiently eased so that I could forget those concerns and typically lose myself in being Alison Riley, the steamroller that thought she was a secretary. I noticed, however, that despite her ambition to make every relationship one of mirth and mischief, Joan's demeanor toward me had significantly tempered; and it wouldn't take a genius to explain why. The awe I felt toward her intellectual abilities was undiminished, but, her becoming childishly indignant over my observations, my suggestions that "performing" with George in the way ;she had intimated fell somehow beyond a benevolent sense of humor, betrayed the fact that maturity was not this creature's strong suit; and as the days went by, and her indignation failed to abate, manifesting itself instead in behavior that resembled nothing more than a permanent tantrum, I know neither if I should feel sorry for her or how I could. The term "temperamental genius" was now a walking, pouting illustration for me to work next to.

George, meanwhile, continued to stop at our workstation to chat with us, and Joan's flirtations with him, as might have been predicted, only gained in intensity. It was obvious that my admonishments had served merely to make her more determined to play with her new toy, as she envisioned George, to spite her surrogate-mother figure, as she saw me. Most of the time I was too busy to pay attention to what went on between these two, but at various times I noticed that they were exchanging little items like books, music tapes and other things. One day I overheard Joan tell George that she wanted to pose topless for some magazine, my guts wrenching inside at the thought of what ideas this might be giving George. On another day they were talking about local venues for music and entertainment, and to my surprise she actually asked him if he'd like to go drinking and dancing at a rock and roll bar she knew of. George practically leaped at the idea, and Joan turned to me, and with exaggerated casualness asked if I'd like to come along; I declined, saying I had a date for that night, and noticed the gleam in George's eyes at the prospect that he might have an evening alone with Joan. But then Joan apparently remembered she had classes that night, which effectively shot down that idea and his hopes. When George left, Joan smiled at me with a look of triumph in her eyes; I pretended to be busy as usual. I thought, if there was anything that Joan enjoyed more than toying with George, it was flaunting these episodes of frustration in front of me. At the same time, I wondered how long Joan could drop all these hints before George would screw up enough confidence to actually ask her out.

The answer came sometime around the end of last November. It was a Friday, the day of the week when a virtually palpable atmosphere of relief and restlessness always seemed to materialize at the firm; that day, when Joan sauntered back from her lunch, the smile on her face was speaking volumes of wickedness.

"Can you believe it, Ali?" she gushed, as she planted herself down on her seat. "George asked me to have dinner with him tonight!"

"No kidding." Oh, no, I thought, it's finally happened. "What did you say?"

"Well, unfortunately I had to turn him down." Joan played absently with the locket that dangled from her neck. "Class tonight."

"Oh." Inwardly, I was thinking, Please, George, take this hint, she's going to have "classes" every night of her life…l

"So he asked if I was free Sunday night, and I said yes!" "You did?"

"Uh huh!" Joan nodded, giggling. "What do you think of that?"

"I guess…that's great." I was actually pretty stunned. What was Joan up to now?

"Yes, we're going to have dinner in a restaurant and then maybe see a movie. George is so funny, he says he wants me to collaborate on a song he's going to write! I think it'll be fun."

"I hope it will be." Both of us returned to our work and spoke little to each other for the rest of the afternoon. I remember being especially surprised that George had actually succeeded in arranging a date with Joan Stevens, and worrying that what he had in mind for their relationship would fall painfully short of what Joan planned. Inside my brain, there was no question that whatever Joan was going to do was nowhere near the best interests of George Kerns.

CHAPTER FOUR

For me, the weekend following the Friday when Joan announced her date with George passed pretty normally. I spent Friday night and most of Saturday visiting my parents in Pennsylvania, then came back to Northern Virginia to my apartment, where I spent more than the usual amount of time practicing my drumming. I hadn't dated anyone myself for months, and I wasn't missing it terribly, other than regretting the fact that I hadn't met anybody that even remotely attracted me. If anything, I was worried that I might never meet a guy that appealed to me, but until I did I wasn't going to waste any time with the many guys I did know, when things like work or drumming seemed to make lots more sense.

When Monday morning came along, and I resumed my weekly routine, I noticed at 9:15 that Joan hadn't come in yet. That wasn't exactly a total surprise, but it amused me to wonder what had happened, and I awarded myself a coffee with extra cream and sugar while juicy theories meandered through my mind. Nine thirty rolled around, and still there was no Joan; "Atta boy, Georgie!" I thought to myself, and I began to expect to be receiving Joan's 'calling in sick' any minute.

Instead, at approximately quarter to ten, Joan made her appearance. The first thing I noticed was that her characteristic blue eyeshadow was missing. Next I noticed that she actually looked tired; and she **wasn't even smiling**. Without her make-up, and looking the way she did, I was almost at a loss for words. All I could manage to say was, "Good morning, Joan."

"Hi." She half-barked, flinging her purse onto her desk and heading immediately for the coffee room. I was so taken aback by this strange new Joan that I was almost scared.

Joan returned from the coffee room blowing into a cup of black coffee. She stood outside our secretarial station, sipped some of her drink, then slowly walked to her chair and sank into it with a sigh. Her silence was unbearable. I had to say something.

"Joan, dare I guess that your date last night wasn't quite as fun as you expected?"

She looked at me with an expression of such unexpected malice that I could feel my heart skip a beat. For a few seconds she didn't say anything. Now I was scared.

"Don't ask." was all she said.

That Monday had to be one of the most tension-filled experiences I ever had, at work or anywhere. My mind virtually ached from having to withhold all the questions swirling within me, I found it even more difficult than ever to concentrate on my work, and if Joan said anything to me all morning long I don't remember it. Whatever had happened had transformed Joan into a sullen zombie-secretary, whose only display of emotion was a marked increase in the rate her eyelids would blink whenever the telephone would ring or she'd move from one assignment to the next. Her boss, Mr. Gibbs, came out of his office, after Joan had stomped off to lunch, and leaned over my desk, his voice a nervous whisper. "Alison, what's the matter with Joan today?"

"I really don't know, Mr. Gibbs, but it must be something terrible. She isn't talking to anyone."

"My God, maybe someone in her family died—or, do you think something could have happened to her? It's so bizarre to see her this way." The pure concern in Mr. Gibbs' wide blue eyes, behind his wire-rimmed spectacles, made me feel ashamed for having been scared by Joan's strange withdrawal. After all, how well did I know George anyway? What if he really had done something—something awful?

"I—tried to talk to her this morning, but she doesn't want to open up about it right now. I think it's best if she just—works it out her own way."

"Well, I hope you know what you're talking about." Mr. Gibbs sighed. "Heaven knows I've lost more than my share of secretaries, but I've never seen any of them as upset as Joan seems today." He gave me a weary, sad smile. "But you girls understand each other much better than I ever will. Please, Alison, if you would try to make her feel better, I'd be so grateful."

I nodded, feeling better for being able to share a bit of human concern, a rather rare occurrence in my world where facts and figures reigned so supreme; now I felt I could at least focus my attention on what I was supposed to be doing. I flicked on my C. R. T. and had just finished centering a title onto its document when I noticed, out of the corner of my eye, somebody standing in front of my workstation.

It was George. He was standing there, grinning his most ecstatic grin, and chomping enthusiastically on a piece of red licorice. "Hi, Alison. How's it goin'?"

"Just fine." I think I managed to appear as if George's ebullience wasn't the most incongruous sight of my day. "What are you so full of piss and vinegar about, today?"

"Oh, I dunno," he chuckled through a mouthful of candy. "Things are just going pretty well for a change. And, of course, it's nice to see you and Joan. By the way, where is the mystery secretary today?"

"She's…" I had to think twice to remember. "…she's out to lunch, and—"

"Oh. Well, I'm sorry I missed her, but would you give this to her for me?" He handed me a sheet of folded loose-leaf paper.

"Sure." I said, not really very sure at all.

"Thanks. I'll see ya later." Off he went, obviously in some kind of euphoria. When he had gone around the corner, I opened the piece of paper. On it was written, in very neat script, the words to a song he had written:

Everly Beverly

Been gone — too long
With no — word of
your condition…
You took — my car
I did — not give
You permission…
Out on — the road
No tel — ling where
You are — heading…
After — I spent
So much — money
On our — wedding…

Screech marks in the driveway,
that's all that's left of my 'Vette
You said you'd be just a sec
But you haven't come back yet

Rush hour will swallow you Detectives will follow you
Helicopters over your Head for cover or you're dead

Bev'rly — my love
How could — you leave
In such — a whirl?
Did you — not say
That you — would
always be — my girl?
And I — believed
That our — love would
Last for — ever…
Instead — I find
That you — have gone
Off to — gether, with

Credit cards, wallet too, petty cash, Daughter Sue

Entering Beverlyville, you take a Beverly pill
Everly Beverly, will you ever be my Bev?

I had no choice, you left me no electives
An all points watch, issued by detectives

Now blood — hounds are
In search — of clues
To your — where'bouts…
Nation — al Guards-
Men have — your photo
de — scription…
Even — your moth-
Er now — is comb-

Ing the — Area…
When you're — alone
Some night — the pos-
se will — scare ya…

Now this was weird, I thought. Definitely not your run of the mill love song. Was this the song Joan was saying that George wanted her to collaborate on? I must have sat for fifteen minutes, reading the strangely metered lyrics, frankly impressed that George could have produced such an imaginative story, and wondering what kind of music was supposed to accompany it. I liked the rhythm, and the way he'd split up the words to fit it:

Ba dum, ba dum, ba dum, ba dum, ba dum, ba dum…

and I tried to imagine how I'd accompany these words, if I were drumming to them:

Ba dum ba di-di, ba dum, ba diddly ba, ba bum, ba bum…

Nah, more high hat, more of a jazz sound…

ka wasshk, ka wasshk, ka bum-bum, bum buddy-bump, bum bum smash!

on my crash cymbal. Hmmm, not bad, I thought. I chuckled a bit to myself, so amused at George's nutty lyrics and my own percussive ideas that all the morning's previous, negative thoughts were forgotten.

The next thing I knew, though, Joan had returned. I noticed right away that she had replaced her make-up, her eyes once more surmounted by their characteristic blue shadow, her cheeks a rosy red. She was even smiling, somewhat sheepishly. She was so much like the old, familiar, invulnerable Joan that, without even thinking, I returned her smile and handed her the paper.

"Here. George Kerns left this for you."

As soon as I had said George's name I knew I had made a mistake. Joan's smile dissolved into the same, malicious grimace I'd trembled at this morning. Her eyes, augmented by their make-up, smoldered insanely like a pair of multi-colored coals. Stiffly, it was the zombie-secretary that snatched the piece of loose-leaf from my hands; her mouth pursed as those deep-blue lids hooded the eyes that scanned George's lyrics. Finally, after perhaps thirty seconds of contemptuous perusal, she wheeled on her high heels and dropped the loose-leaf into her wastebasket.

"If that's his idea of a joke, I'm afraid I don't get it." she said, dropping into her seat, her back as straight as a board.

"I think he meant it as a song for you. I thought you liked George." "I thought so, too, until last night!" she snapped back.

"Why, what happened last night?"

"I told you—". Horrified, I saw that she was actually gritting her teeth at me. Then, as she saw how her anger was distressing me, she composed herself with an exaggeratedly condescending effort, into the emotionless mask she'd been wearing all day, ludicrous as the effect was, not what her face wore all of her "mystery secretary" make-up. "Just don't ask." she finally muttered, and silently, studiously, she took a pencil from her drawer and proceeded to proofread a document.

Embarrassed, confused, and especially, hurt, I stared helplessly at the wastebasket that contained the song I had thought was so clever.

It was my turn to take lunch, although food was as far from my mind as any hope of understanding the trauma my catatonic neighbor was going through. For all of my intentions to be the perfect working machine, there was no way I could function oblivious as a person I knew was in pain, regardless of how that pain had been inflicted. If there's one thing I simply can't understand, it's how anyone could be that cold. I picked up my purse and wandered away, confused to the point of stupidity by all these things I'd never thought could have involved me, these things that had somehow dwarfed me and my little world of altruistic, no-nonsense responsibility.

All I can remember of my lunch hour that day was walking out onto the street, merging into the thronging masses that stalk purposefully up and down the sidewalks; losing myself in the loneliness and depression that always came on when I couldn't think of anything better to do than something like this. When an hour of this aimlessness had elapsed, and I'd shambled back to my desk, at least i was too hungry from not eating to care much about the force- field of hypersensitivity that still crackled around my work area. Joan acknowledged me with a terse tightening of her lips, and in reprisal I nodded, slung my purse onto my chairback, and joined her at the Workstation of Dread. With an effort that would have been hopeless were it not for years of experience, I lifted my hands to my keyboard and engrossed myself in a program that didn't need to be started until the following day; knowing that it was only a matter of hours until George would return to visit the woman who had thrown his song into the trash.

He appeared at four o'clock, the time he was scheduled to leave for the day. There was no way I could have prepared myself for the confrontation between the light-hearted office services assistant and the diametrically unsympathetic object of his affections. He sauntered up to the desk where Joan had her head lowered over a newspaper, resolutely shutting herself off from the world, pretending to be completely fixed upon the comics section, during a lull in her usually hectic schedule. Smiling munificently, maddeningly ignorant of the horror he was so blithely about to detonate, I watched as he waited for Joan to look up from her reading.

"So." he ventured, when it was apparent mere friendly presence would be insufficient to merit her greeting, "What did you think of the song?"

Her face rose, flushing a red that nearly matched the blusher on her cheeks. For an agonizing, protracted space of time, her eyes blinked furiously, and I was struck speechless as, separated as I was by a few feet, I nevertheless felt the brunt of the bizarre climb of blood pressure surging withing her. Finally, those red, red lips parted, words blasted through set teeth that barely allowed speech to issue, and the sound that came was infused with the purest hate anyone could loathe to encounter.

"I thought it was gross."

I didn't know how much of George's reaction I missed from being unable to watch. I did see his features fall from happy expectation to what looked like he was going to throw up.

"Uhhh…" he stuttered, his face draining of color, his hands fumbling at his sides. I felt like I was going to cry out of hysteria, as each of these two people plummeted through such extreme, irrational emotional states that I wanted to yell "Stop!"; but I didn't. Instead, I found that I couldn't continue to bear Joan's merciless, unrelentling, inhumanly horrid image any longer, and blinking against my tears, I turned to see George, his lips trembling with the humiliation that all but paralyzed him, stutter out his last words of defense.

"It's—it's just a song."

He didn't look to see if his words had any effect, but walked quickly away, his face hidden from sight, his footsteps desperate to flee the hot silence that remained between Joan and me.

CHAPTER FIVE

I didn't do anything. I didn't flirt with anybody, I didn't try to hurt anybody, I didn't do anything that I wouldn't have done any day of the week for as long as I can remember. As near as I could figure, the only thing that tied me in with the conflict between Joan Stevens and George Kerns was advising Joan against it in the first place; I had to keep reminding myself that there was no way I could have known that there would be this kind of a result; I had to, because the events of that awful Monday sank me into the most severe depression of my life.

I walked to the Metro station that day, and suddenly it seemed, as if it had dawned on me for the first time, how utterly alone I was, in the crowds, the crowds that surrounded me for as far as my eye could see and my mind could imagine; crowds of cars, crowds of people, crowds of buildings, everything else was so much, and so big, and so remote; and I was so small, and only one. The feelings of alienation and impotence wouldn't go away, but grew and grew as I made my way home, seeing all the same things I'd see every night, and dwelling on the dismal conviction that none of them saw me. I was tired, and hungry, and that afternoon I'd seen two people bring each other to a level of misery so idiotically pathetic that it made me a pathetic idiot. That's how profoundly the emnity between George and Joan overruled my usually carefree state of mind.

When I unlocked my apartment door that night I felt like I was opening my own drawer at the morgue, loading myself in with a tag on my toe. I didn't bother to switch on the lights, but instead flopped onto the couch and stared at my drum set, ghostily lit by the meager glow from the street that ebbed, red and brass, through my living room window. As everything else in the world had so suddenly decided, even my drum set was ignoring me; no more of its usual coaxing to please make some noise; it just sat there, dumber than a rabbit, too dumb to even glitter very much. After a few minutes, when I realized that I was bemoaning the loss of intelligent mental communication with my drum set, I finally broke down and cried the cry I'd been saving since four o'clock that afternoon, cried and sobbed into my pillow until I felt much better and went into the kitchen and ate a lot of ice cream with M & M's in it and went to sleep.

When I went back to work the next day, I felt about as apathetic toward society as somebody could without wanting to commit suicide. My little one percent of individual personality was, for all intents and purposes, as lost as it seemed that the idea of goodwill towards men had gotten lost, somewhere in the process that had brought me to this point. Which isn't to say that my work suffered for this; no, I was still quite able to carry on due to the sheer momentum my career had developed, in fact you might say that the absence of one percent of my being only meant that now I could devote one hundred percent to the cause of the firm. It wouldn't be true, but you could say that.

After the humiliating encounter between him and Joan, George didn't come around our workstation to say hello anymore. For a few days, knowing that I wasn't liable to see him coming by for his friendly little visits was a difficult thing to put out of my mind. Joan, on the other hand, was back to her old self by the following day, with the exception that she wouldn't talk to me anymore beyond "Hello", "I'm going to lunch", "I'm going to the bathroom" and "Good Night". But beyond this, she resumed her role as the secretarial life of the party, her streams of admirers flowing unabated, her orgiastic laughter resounding anew in the halls. Mr. Gibbs thanked me for whatever I did to cheer her up, and of course didn't get my joke when I said it was nothing. As days turned into weeks, I stopped having to think about these things, and started to take it for granted that George would never come around to say "Hi" and Joan was going to ignore me, and rule the world, forever.

The weather got colder as December came along, and my depression slowly fell away as the effects of winter drew me, and the people around me, into all those situations that make you glad for human companionship, like snow-bound streets that drive everyone indoors, and having to get all bundled up to stay warm, and the whole new meaning of a cup of coffee when it's so cold that you can see your breath. Every day my co-workers and I would come in from the outside, our shoes wet with slush, stamping our feet and rubbing our hands, sharing in the feeling of unity that our common struggle against the winter elements brought us. And one other very influential factor was fueling the enthusiasm that I and my fellow workers were enjoying; the annual Christmas Party, as announced in the colorful pamphlets distributed to our desks and tacked up in the coffee rooms by the Office Services department. With all my work to take care of, and all these other winter goings-on, I found my optimism and my sense of humor becoming as close to completely restored as working next to The Joan Show could allow.

Around the middle of December came a forebodingly grey-skied Wednesday, and the word had spread from the televisions at home and the radios at work that the Federal Government was going to send its workers home early to avoid a rush-hour disaster when the season's first major blizzard promised to strike in the afternoon. The firm traditionally followed the government's lead in these matters and gave us administrative leave, announced over our computer screens. Sometime near twelve o'clock that Wednesday the announcement came over my C. R. T. that the building would close at two o'clock and that all employees were expected to leave by that time. As the cheers of my fellow secretaries cascaded around me, I myself was cursing under my breath, because I had hours of dictation to type up, and had been planning to stock up on my supplies after that, which would take another hour for filling out the requisition form, going to the supply room, and waiting for George to put it all together. I looked at my empty box of letterhead stationery, my cup nearly bereft of pens and pencils, my cupboard that needed typewriter ribbons and paper clips and staples and scotch tape and maybe fifteen other sundry, essential items; and then I thought of the prospect of coming to work, on the morning after a snow emergency, and asked myself, would I rather come back to a secretarial station all stocked up and ready to go but with a lot of dictation to type, or would I rather have the dictation half-done and come in to a desk that reeked of poverty?

I was sure that my boss would prefer that the dictation took priority, and my own nature wanted to get it over-with; but a gaggle of secretaries and a couple of men were loitering around Joan's desk, reveling over the early dismissal and speculating how long the unexpected vacation would last, and under the distracting circumstances I knew that a transcription job would take probably as long as normal, if not more, while frustrating and angering me all along.

On the other hand, if I filled out a requisition form and took it to the supply room, I'd circumvent all that and be able to visit George, whom I hadn't seen for more than two weeks, and no doubt could use an encouraging word. After all my years of faithful service, I reasoned that Mr. Carruthers would certainly understand how the snow emergency had delayed his transcription, vital as it was. With these rationales, I opened my desk drawer, withdrew a pink requisition form from a manila folder, and started to list the many items my near-bankrupt area needed. When I was done, about forty- five minutes later, the commotion around Joan's desk and echoing from down the hall had risen ticklishly in fervor, as snow could be seen drifting against the dusky grey outside our windows and everyone scurried to finish their day's business and "exodus" the building.

I walked to the supply room, passing a few of my co-workers bundled in scarves and woolen hats and gloves, all happily trundling outside and wishing me a happy holiday; I thanked them and returned the sentiments, thinking about my drum set that had been waiting dormantly for so long, waiting to be played, and how, though there might be a happier way to spend a holiday, I still hadn't met him. Ha, ha, I thought, now I knew my one percent was still around, skulking inside my heart; and to make double-sure of it, I indulged myself in a little fantasy as I neared the supply room, a reverie involving a crackling fireplace, a bearskin rug and gentle but masterful hands…

"Hello." The next thing I knew, George Kerns was staring expectantly at me from the other side of the supply room window. The contrast was so abrupt from what I'd been daydreaming that I jumped, for a moment alarmed that he had caught me without my clothes on.

"Uhhh…" I managed to reply, as I remembered that I was at work, all my clothes were as they should be, and what did I come here for? Oh, yeah, supplies, I grinned sheepishly to recall.

"You sound like me." he noted, returning my smile. "But it could be worse. You could look like me." I laughed, happy to see old trustworthy George in his quiet, simple supply room. He looked happy to see me, too, and for a moment I wondered how lonely his life got, removed from the society of all the professionals and secretaries and operating out of this dark little room full of boxes of paper and pens eight hours a day, five days a week.

"Hi, George, how've you been? You're looking well." Actually, even though the last time I saw him he'd looked like he needed to find a place to vomit in privacy, compared to the merry mood that filled everyone else I'd seen that day, George looked like a graphic example of "something that the cat dragged in". His eyes, which at their best reminded me of a close-up of Bela Lugosi's in Dracula, were sad and fatigued-looking, the skin below them, lined and dark.

His clothes were wrinkled and not very clean, and his hair looked like it needed twenty dollars of repair.

"Same as ever." he replied, "And if I'm not looking well, things must be awful tough for you these days. Need some supplies?"

"Yes, thanks." I handed him the pink sheet and shifted from trying to overlook his grunginess, to offering some commiseration. "I haven't seen you in weeks. I've missed you."

"Oh, yes, I'm sure." he raised his voice, with not a little bitter sarcasm, as he went to his shelves and started loading my supplies into an empty copier-paper box.

"No, really, I have. I haven't seen you since that day you gave me your song."

"I meant for you to give it to Joan. Did she even read it?" "I think so." It felt weird to open the subject of that fiasco. "Did you read it?"

"Uh huh!" I replied enthusiastically, seeing a chance to cheer him up. "I thought it was very clever."

"You're kidding." he smirked morosely.

"No, really, I'm not. I liked the rhythm of it." Sensing his skepticism, I reinforced my praise. "And that was a funny story. Who the heck is 'Everly Beverly'? That's so cute."

"Cute, huh?" I could tell he was pleased, as an ironic grin spread across his face. "A girl dumps a guy, takes all his money and his car and his daughter after they got married so he'll probably end up paying alimony if he ever finds her and meanwhile his heart's completely broken." He shook his head in comic despair. "That's about as cute as a tarantula."

"More like a black widow!" I pointed out, seeing how I'd succeeded in getting him to lighten up, and hoping that by showing more than passing attention to his song he could be really discouraged. "Joan told me you write music. Did you write some music for that song?"

"Uh huh. Yeah. Sort of. Maybe not what you'd call music. More like—ambient audio-psychosis."

"Ha ha! That sounds neat." I put on my most convincing, feminine smile. "I'd like to hear it."

"Really? Just like Joan?"

Whoops. Careful, Alison, remember your male-ego lessons.

They're big as balloons, but all it takes is a pin-prick…

"No, not at all like Joan." I could see by his expression that I'd lost some ground. Time for even more sincerity. "George, I don't know what happened between you and her, but I know it wasn't your song that made her do what she did."

"Yeah, well…I'd like to know what did."

"Is there something that happened when you two went out to dinner a couple of weeks ago?"

I knew the question was probing at the crux of his misery. George stopped loading items into the copier-paper box and stared at me, his wounded eyes scanning my own silently for confirmation of a soul he could trust, and just as wordlessly I blinked back that here it was. "So you know about our dinner date?" he asked finally.

"Yes, Joan tells me—that is, she used to tell me everything. Then you two went out on that date, and she hasn't talked to me since." I noted how he took this all in, how he hadn't taken his eyes from the box of supplies he had loaded, as if there were a weight on his shoulders he wanted desperately to be rid of, but was powerless to do so on his own. "George, I know some things about Joan that I don't think you know, and if you want to talk about it—" When I paused, he lifted pained, glazed eyes to meet mine, then looked away. "If you don't want to talk about it, I'll be glad to just mind my own business."

George drew a heavy sigh and rolled his eyes to the ceiling. "I think— it is my considered opinion that Joan Stevens is a test that God put into my life to see how much agony I can take." The force, and the resigned tone, of his words struck me that he wasn't exaggerating, the truth of his statement was real and definitely spoke of the misery she had caused him. When, after a few seconds, he looked at me again to see my reaction, my compassionate expression beseeched him to open up more; he grimaced bravely, and I knew that it would take a great deal of strength for him to share what must have been a tragic experience for him.

I had already committed what I felt was a mistake by trying to advise Joan against getting involved with George; that was why I felt apprehensive now, offering myself as a sounding-board to him. From the intensity of his emotions now, however, it seemed to me that he had no idea that Joan had never felt attracted to him in the first place, and that, knowing Joan as I did, I was sure that all her alleged interests in him had sprung from her wanting to outrage me. Much as the knowledge of this might disappoint him, I was sure that it would spare him the agony he spoke of when he learned that the woman he had wasted so much heartbreak over, in reality, fell into the "If you can't say something nice about somebody, don't say anything at all" category.

"George, like I said, if you don't want to talk about it, that's fine with me. Joan doesn't want to talk about it, and that's fine too. I've been working here for three years and never gotten involved with anybody's personal problems, and I'm convinced that that's the only way to get work done. But that doesn't mean I can't tell when something's so wrong that, if I didn't bend the rules a little bit, something more important than business will suffer." George nodded to indicate he was listening, and I smiled at our mutual seriousness. "Look, what I'm saying is I can tell you you're really strung out over Joan, and I don't blame you after what she did; and the way everything happened, it seems like there must have been something strange that happened to make her thrash you out like that." George kept on nodding receptively; I was getting tired of doing all the talking, but I sensed that I was getting some good accomplished. "Yes?" Something strange happened? Talk to me, George."

"Yes, something "strange" happened. But, look, it's a really long story, and I'm not sure you want to hear about it."

"Okay, George. I understand. But there is something about Joan I think you should know, and that's not a very long story—"

"Yeah, well, did you happen to see what time it is?"

"Oh my gosh, it's ten to two. I've got to get all these things back to my desk."

"Yeah. Well, look, Alison, I've got my own ideas about Joan and everything and I don't know about how I want someone else involved."

"Involved?" Involved in what? That's my point, George, you're all trashed out over something that's…well, not even worth thinking about."

"Oh yeah? I think that's for me to decide, don't you?"

"Not when you don't know all the facts, George." I was starting to get irritated at the rate our logics were chasing each other's tails, while time was running out for us to vacate the building.

"Okay, George, I only wanted to help. I'm sure you'll work things out one way or the other. I've really got to go. See ya."

"Alison, wait." George called out as I grabbed my box of supplies. "Look, I'm really grateful to you for wanting to help. I'm not sure I would be able to work this out myself. Do you think maybe we could talk about this—tonight, maybe? Like, maybe go out to a restaurant, I'll buy you dinner. If you're not busy?"

"Well…seeing how I was going to work here this afternoon, and that's completely out of the question now…but I don't want to stay in D. C., either, with the snow and everything. There's a lot of nice restaurants out in Richardson, near where I live. What do you think of having dinner out there?

"That sounds great! I live just a couple of Metro stops out from Richardson, myself. Wow, all this time, and I didn't know we were practically neighbors."

"I guess that's because you work the eight to four schedule and I work the nine to five. Otherwise we'd have seen each other on the Metro."

"Yeah…" George murmured, his mind apparently boggling at this new-found coincidence. "Weird."

"Well, we'd better get going, there's only about five minutes left before they close the building."

George grabbed his coat and scarf and shut off the lights in the supply room. "I'll meet you downstairs in the lobby, outside the elevators." he said, and I nodded, carrying the heavy load of supplies back to my workstation. I set the box under my desk, got my coat and gloves and turned off Mr. Carruther's office lights. As I made my way to rendevous with George, I couldn't help comparing how my evening's prospects differed from the idealized daydream I'd had earlier, and sighed, thinking that at least this beat spending the evening with my long-neglected drum set.

CHAPTER SIX

When we stepped out of the building, snow was falling heavily, and there was at least a couple of inches of it on the sidewalk, while on the streets it lay in random, dirty stripes and patches in areas that cars hadn't driven and turned it into rivers of cold black ice-water. The air was thick with the cold and the blizzarding snow, and through it the visibility had been lowered so much that the cars and people struggling to get home seemed like mere dark shapes on the background of inclement white precipitation. With his red scarf pulled up over his mouth, George's words were a muffled shout against the street noises, which were intensified by the increased density of the air. "C'mon, let's get out of here." Eager as he to vacate the eskimo pie that D. C. was, I fell into step beside him and we hurriedly stalked through the storm to the Metro station down the street.

Once we had gone down the escalator to join the wet, impatient crowd waiting for the train, George pulled his scarf from his mouth and smiled at me as I stamped my wet shoes against the hexagonal bricks that made up the station's platform. "Most of the time these days I'm too busy to notice, but every once in a while I really like to take a few minutes to admire these Metro stations." he said.

"Yeah, me too. They remind me of something out of a science fiction movie about a post nuclear disaster."

"Ha ha." he laughed. "They don't strike me quite so depressingly. I know a guy who's the brother of my ex-girlfriend, and he used to be a surveyor, and he used to go down in these stations when they were nothing but big tunnels in the ground and work with the digging crews. To look at these stations now is impressive enough, but trying to appreciate how much work went into them is almost impossible for me."

"You had a girlfriend?" I asked, not as eager to marvel over the architectural history of the Metro system as I was surprised to hear George mention his liaison.

"You sound as if that's hard to believe." he observed self-deprecatingly. "Okay, maybe it is." he went on, turning his gaze to the mouth of the subway tunnel where the train would come. "I've changed a lot since we broke up, and not a lot for the better."

"Was she pretty?"

"Yes. She was beautiful. She had long, strawberry blonde hair that went down to her—uhhh…" His face spread into the first mischievous smile I'd seen him wear in weeks. "I went out with her for almost six years. That's longer than most people stay married. Then she went and left me and ran off with a guy I knew, actually I thought he was a real good friend." The lights set into the concrete edge of the platform began to flash, signaling that the train was about to arrive.

"That sounds pretty awful." I commiserated, thinking it really sounded like the typical tragic story I'd been trying for the umpteenth time to avoid at the coffee room; but I couldn't deny that six years was an impressive length of time for somebody, especially George, to have a relationship, in the callous, shallow society that the eighties had engendered. Upon reflection, however, the idea of George having a girlfriend itself was somewhat beyond "impressive"; but if it were true, then it seemed to make a lot of sense that it would have been a deep, long-lasting relationship. I thought of what kind of girl would live a guy like George, and wondered what kind of life they shared…

The train was pulling into the station, with its headlights, two blazing balls of white, and the rising roar of the motor and the wheels against the tracks. George, the crowd, and I turned to face the platform, preparing to board the train. It was then that I heard a most unexpected sound, a sad, world-weary drawl, and I looked at George and saw that, as he stood staring at the train braking to a stop in front of us he was singing, in a low tone, slowly mouthing words that were cutting through all the extraneous noise:

When the train…come in the station…
It had two lights…on behi-i-ind…

I recognized the classic Robert Johnson song, "Love In Vain", from an old Rolling Stones album I used to listen to. It was intriguing to hear George singing like a heartbroken Negro, and strange, too, that he would just open up and start singing, subdued as the grumbling sound was. Though he didn't look at me, as we entered the train and took seats next to each other, I didn't want to take my eyes off of him as his little blues rendition droned on:

You know, it's hard to tell, it's hard to tell…
When all-l-l-l yer lo-o-ove's in vainnn…

"That's really pretty, George."

"Yeah, I was pretty strung out for about a whole year after I broke up with her." he said, returning to his normal, more grating speaking voice. "It was one of those relationships that I thought I couldn't get over, you know, "I'll never find a woman like you again", "I might as well be dead", seeing her face everywhere from first thing in the morning to last thing at night, all that stuff."

"But it sounds like you managed to get over it."

"Yeah, I did." He paused, and then he looked at me. "It was utterly impossible, there was no way in the world was I going to find a girl that could take the place of her, I was despairing that I had lost her and I was despairing that there was no way to find her. I was hopeless. Hopeless! Believe me, you'll never know how hopeless I was. I sure don't." I looked up at his face, the one that I and everybody else knew made a policy of avoiding, and wondered how much pain the person behind it had gone through, was still going through, pain that never came to the surface; even if it did, as the intimation of it was coming now, who would notice, or care? Anybody could understand that these emotions George was confessing had to be contained, buried, forgotten, in order to carry on and lead a semblance of a happy life; up until now, I knew that is what he'd been doing.

But George was still too strange to me, too much the shunned office services assistant, for me to really empathize with the hopelessness he spoke of, and it bothered me that I couldn't, but when you can't, you can't, so no use dwelling on it. I nodded, and said, "I'm sorry. No, I guess I never will understand. But you must realize how damaging it is to feel that way, don't you? You know, you only live once? Life's too short? Plenty of fish in the sea? I haven't got time for the pain?"

George nodded. "Yes, but there's a difference between knowing full well that you've got to fix your car and having the money to do it. But look," he interjected, with a shake of his head, "The point is that I have gotten over her."

"That's good. A year is way too long to waste mooning over somebody."

"You're right. There's only one problem." he said with an ironic grimace, as I noticed that we were arriving at my station.

"What's that?"

"The person that I found—that made me forget all about my ex-girlfriend?"

"Uh-huh?"

"Joan."

"I really wanted to laugh. George goes through all that serious soap opera material, and then throws in Joan Stevens as the solution to all his problems. It seemed as outlandish a concept as the ideas that made me spasm out in grocery lines, and I think I concealed my mirth just about as effectively as I did in those situations, this time by taking a big handful of my thigh flesh and squeezing. Hard.

"Oh, George." I managed to say when I had sufficiently quelled myself, and we rose to exit the car. "Now I know I've got to tell you something."

We exited the station, returning to the forbidding elements that were blanketing the streets, and walked in silence a couple of blocks until we came to a restaurant that served good, inexpensive Italian food.

"How's this look?" I asked.

"Looks good to me." George assented, and we entered and chose a table in a somewhat private booth. The waitress came, took our orders for a couple of burger plates and coffees, and I started to reopen our conversation.

"George, if you're at all interested in Joan Stevens, I think you ought to know that she isn't interested in you."

"I sort of got that impression." George replied. "But what I don't understand is what made her change so suddenly. One day were getting along great, and then Bam. The next day she hated my guts." "Yes, well, maybe that's what it looked like to you, but the fact is —"—the moment of the big bomb—" She was never interested in you."

"Huh?"

"George, Joan Stevens led you on. She was toying with you. She might have thought you were an amusing little distraction, but the only reason she flirted with you so much was to make me mad."

"What?"

"That's right. She was saying she thought you were a funny guy to tease, and when I tried to tell her that that wasn't such a good idea, she decided to take advantage of you, to get me pissed off."

"Uhhh…"

"George, Joan Stevens has nothing on her mind but lots of men with lots of little zeroes on their paychecks. For you to be concerned with her is more stupid than I can describe. Forget her. If anything,

you should hate her, but the best thing is to forget her. She doesn't exist. She's nothing but bad news."

George sat, staring sullenly out of the window at the snow, for a few minutes, taking this all in. The waitress returned without food, and I commenced eating my burger, feeling I could really enjoy it now that my duty had been done. George would recuperate, and things would return to normal again; I began to look forward to seeing him waving "Hi" and pushing his cart past my desk while we both ignored Joan.

Instead, George turned to me and said, "I can't forget her. I still care for her."

"Don't be ridiculous." I scoffed through a mouthful of burger.

"I'm not. You don't know what happened between me and her, especially that night we had our date."

"I don't need to!" Please, George, don't be doing this, I'm telling you for your own good. "I know for a fact that she thinks you're a joke." Oh, brother, what a way to try to cheer a guy up.

"Maybe that's absolutely true." he replied, also through a mouthful of food. "And so what? In a way she's right to think so. I am a joke. If my life were a fan it would be covered with shit!"

"Spmmpph!" I couldn't help laughing.

"But look, Alison, that night with Joan was the most wonderful night of my life. I never felt—I haven't felt so happy since I broke up with my old girlfriend. It was impossible. It was hopeless. But Joan did it. She made me forget my old girlfriend."

"Okay." I replied, certain that I was the only person capable of rational thought in the booth. "So that ought to tell you that there's someone out there that can make you forget Joan, too." And don't look at me, I remember thinking…"

"Perhaps it would. And maybe I'm crazy, like a starving man that you just gave a hamburger. But Joan went even further than just make me forget my old girlfriend."

"Like how?"

"Well, of course you'd have to be there." George qualified, serious as ever. "A lot happened that night. We went to a restaurant, and she told me all kinds of things about herself, and I did the same about myself. Then we went to a movie, and that was good…and then we went back to my place, and I got out my guitar and played some of my songs for her."

"Does she sing very well?"

"I don't know. She didn't sing. I'd say she's one of those people that doesn't have to sing well, with everything else going for her." George finished his burger and took a sip of his coffee. "But she seemed to really like my songs, and didn't make fun of the way I sing."

"You do put a lot of sincerity into it." I commented, remembering "Love In Vain" in the subway.

"Yeah, well, anyway, uhhh…the thing is, most of the night she just sat quietly, being friendly and sympathetic and everything, and so maybe I was just convincing myself that here I was with the most beautiful, wonderful girl in the world, because that's what I wanted to think; maybe everything she did say wasn't the most inspiring conversation in the world, and it was just my super-intensified wishful thinking that made it seem like it was; but what happened was, almost like I couldn't stop myself, around the time it was starting to get late, when I'd put down my guitar and she put some music on the stereo—I leaned over and started kissing her."

"You what?" It was my turn to be shocked. George Kerns kissed Joan Stevens? I'd sooner put my hand in a garbage disposal.

"Yes."

"What did she do?"

"Well, uhhh…" His face broke into an embarrassed smile. "Of course, it's kind of impossible to describe, but—well, I went out with my old girlfriend for six years, and what Joan did was better." His eyes rolled up and he adopted an expression of intense reconsideration. "Preferable. Definitely preferable."

"Oh for crying out loud."

"I did a couple of times." he added calmly.

"Well, that puts a new light on matters." I admitted, "But that doesn't really change my point. It just means that she wanted to lead you on as far as possible, and then she certainly did. You've got to see that, George. Invent a good word for her, like tramp, strumpet, sleaze-bucket, and insert it into your vocabulary. Use often."

"Alison, I can't. I just can't. I've got this theory as for why. I was raised a Catholic. Are you a Catholic?"

"Well, I was raised one."

"Well, then you can understand my point. It has to do with my upbringing, the way Catholics put the Fear of God in you right from the beginning, when you're seven years old, and they put you into these catechism classes and they drill you and drill you, again and again, love your neighbor, forgive your enemy, turn the other cheek, if someone sins against you, you hate their sins but you love them." George drained his coffee cup, as I had mine. "In essence, by the time you're grown up, and trying to make a living comes around, they've rendered you utterly unprepared for the real world."

"Are you telling me that you could possibly overlook what Joan's done because of something you learned in catechism when you were seven years old?"

"Absolutely. My programming was set when I was below the age of reason. It's too late now, I'll never be able to respond in self-defense like ninety-nine percent of the world does. Get that through your head, Alison. I can't hate anybody. Too much education. And besides—speaking of education—the way she—she showed me…things like I never imagined a girl could—would—"

"Okay, George, I get the picture." I frowned at him. "But if you're going to hang on to the idea of Joan being anything better than a ball-busting bimbo you're on your way to a worse racking than you already got. If that's possible. Is that what you want?"

"No." was all he said; but looking at me with those helpless eyes, drowning in their noble, obsolete ideals, I was utterly at a loss for any further criticism. I pursed my lips and shook my head at him. "George." I sighed. "What can be done for you? You and the Catholic Church."

"I don't know." he offered meekly. "I'd like to cheer up. That would help a lot. I used to be happy all the time, until my luck kind of went bad."

"Yeah, maybe that's it." I looked at my watch, which said it was about three-thirty. "Well, gee, it's still kind of early. What do you like to do for fun?"

"Fun?" George seemed to brighten up considerably. "Well, I guess I like to go bowling, or maybe go to a movie, or camp out, you know." "Um hmm." It was so good to change the subject, and see some light in George's eyes; and I think his mention of good old Catholicism must have brought out a bit of the Good Samaritan in me; in any case, a rather wild idea was trying to surface from deep inside of me, where my good old one percent had made its presence known earlier that day. "And you do like to write music, too, don't you?"

"Well, yeah, though I haven't been able to write anything in a while. You know how it is, when you're depressed."

"Yeah, sort of. I've got an idea." Knowing George as I did, I made sure to present it as coolly as possible. "How would you like to come by and see my apartment?"

"Well, that sounds real nice. I'd love to. Maybe we could play some chess, or do you like to watch T. V., or, uhhh…"

"Actually, I've got something else in mind. Sort of a surprise." Listen to me, I thought. If it had been almost any male other than George I was making this proposition to, he'd have to be awfully cute and I'd have to be feeling awfully naughty. "But I think this just might get your mind off of Joan." Whoa, I thought, he'd better not get the wrong idea…"

"Okay, sure."

We left the restaurant, walking the two blocks to my apartment, George obviously in a much more positive mood, and I virtually trembling inside at the realization that for the first time, I was going to show somebody my drum set.

CHAPTER SEVEN

When George walked into my living room his face lit up like a little kid's at Christmas.

"Holy Ned!" he gawked, through his scarf. He jerked it down from his mouth, his eyes bulging and blinking in disbelief.

"Do you like it?" I asked coyly, unbuttoning my coat while barely containing the pride welling up within me.

"Uh yep."

"Alison! I had no idea…!" he gasped, standing stock still in the middle of my rug, half-covered with dripping, melting snow, but utterly oblivious to it. He started to walk closer to my glittering, deep blue kit, but I stopped him.

"Wait a minute. Get out of that dripping thing of yours before you get it all wet." George shed his coat, and as I hung it in the hall closet, he walked up to my drums, his mouth hanging open like a mesmerized worshipper, running his fingers over the steel rims that I had kept polished to a mirror brilliance, his eyes ogling over the brilliant brass of the shells. "Oh, Alison…" he murmured reverently, and I laughed a little bit, because you'd think he was gazing at the ceiling of the Sistine Chapel, and not a rather ordinary, five-piece Ludwig drum set; but at the same time, I too felt inordinately proud and joyful and glad that I had spent so much time polishing the rims and the stands and the cymbals. While any other day I never would have thought to show my drums to anyone, now I felt so happy, revealing my greatest secret to George, that I knew I had done not only the right thing, but a wonderful thing. I had to wipe at my eyes just a bit; luckily he didn't notice.

"Do you play them?"

"A little. I turn on the radio sometimes and try to kind of blend in." I walked over, behind the set, and picked up my sticks from the window sill. I kind of waved them nervously, almost afraid to hit the skins. "I haven't played them in a while." I was too embarrassed to say how long, or why.

"So you don't play with a group?"

"No. You're the only one who knows I've even got them." "God. What a waste."

"Oh, I don't think so. It's a real good hobby, I can take out my aggressions. I really enjoy just playing them by myself."

"Come on, Alison, you can't just play drums all by yourself." "Yes I can."

"Nobody does that! Even Buddy Rich has to jam with Johnny Carson's band every once in a while!"

"I guess that makes me different!" I laughed, and just for emphasis I blew off a quick roll from my floor tom to my tom tom, back to floor tom, and Crash! on my cymbal.

"Hey, you're real good!" George exclaimed. "Do that again!"

I'm sure I was blushing awfully, but suppressed the urge to laugh and translated it instead into my unique interpretation of John Bonham's intro to "Rock and Roll", something I'd been practicing for months:

Bam ba-ba-Bam Bam, ba Bam ba-ba-Bam Bam, ba Bam ba-ba- Bam Bam Bam ba-Bam Bam, Bam Bam bambambambambambambam Crash!

"I can't carry on like that too long, or the neighbors'll call the cops." George sat down on the couch, shaking his head. "This is incredible." he muttered. "God, this is the last thing I would have expected! Alison Riley, the perfect employee, the girl who always comes to work early and never misses a day. The one everybody is so busy talking about, but never says a thing herself. All this time—" he hit his forehead with his palm—"all this time everybody thought John Bonham had died, he's been living in Virginia under the cover of Alison Riley, the ultimate secretary!"

"Well, thanks George, but I'm not that good. I've only been playing about a year. I can't read music. All I know is what I've picked up from playing along with the radio."

"Yeah, but c'mon, Alison, you know you're good! I know you're good! What do you think it would sound like if I tried to play "Rock and Roll"? he asked, mugging and jabbing a finger at his chest.

"Ha ha ha!" he looked so crazy and determined, I rocked off my throne laughing. "I don't know, why don't you show me?" I handed him my sticks.

"Are you ready for a little spaz-music in the night?" He straddled my throne, making it squeak frighteningly under his weight, and suddenly it lurched backwards. My months of experience had warned me, though, and I caught him before he sprawled backwards and knocked himself silly.

"Ha ha ha!" I burst out again. "It looks like you've been practicing this spaz-music!"

"God, what's the matter with this thing?" he sputtered as I helped him right himself; waving his arms around madly, his behavior reminded me of a beetle flailing its legs desperately, helplessly upended on its back; and for a moment, I felt a jolt of sympathy for George that was so strong, my head felt light when I realized it was there. My hands didn't want to leave his shoulders, at least until he was looking up at me for a few seconds. "I'm okay, now. Thanks."

I smiled, as a nurse might smile at her patient. "That's a drum throne, George, it's only got three legs."

"Oh. Well, this is how I play the drums." He raised both arms, and to my surprise, spun the sticks through his fingers. "What was that request? Oh, yeah, "Rock and Roll"! Here goes!"

The ensuing clamor was so instantly cacophonous my hands flew to grab his wrists out of sheer instinct for lease-preservation.

"George! Please! That's awful!" I yelled at him. "For crying out loud, where do you think we are, anyway?"

"I'm sorry." The instant he had yelled "Here goes!" he had looked the happiest I'd ever seen him, in fact, "happy" doesn't even begin to describe the look of—well, sheer maniacal frenzy sounds about right. Now, as I gently released my grip on his arms, he looked as shamefully sorrowful as a basset hound. I realized that he was again starting to affect me, in that jolting, sympathetic way, and the knowledge of this was beginning to confuse me, making me wonder, just how much of this man was an open, defenseless wound that depended on others to heal him? Was this why I had asked him to visit me and my drum set? Did the real me really want to…to…

No, I thought, these are ridiculous thoughts. He's a little clumsy, he's had bad luck with girls, and he can't play the drums to save his life. I smiled at him, and said, "Don't worry. You're just a bit too enthusiastic for where we are. But I think we'd better do something else."

"Yeah, okay." Somewhat sheepishly, he relinquished the throne, catching a glimpse of the snow falling outside my window. "Maybe I'd better go home, before it gets too deep outside."

"Do you think so? I didn't want to seem eager for him to leave, for fear that he'd take it the wrong way. In fact, now that he knew about my drums, I felt a little scared to just let him walk out the door with my secret; and even more, once he left, I'd be alone, and for all his weirdness George was a lot more fun than being alone. "Oh, don't go just yet, George, let's talk a while. Would you like a soda?"

"Yeah, sure." I went and got us a couple of cans of soda, glasses and ice out of the icebox, and poured ourselves a pair of drinks on the living room table. "Well, you know, Alison, maybe I can't play guitar, and write music." George continued, his voice sounding like he was trying to get to a point.

"Yes?" I prompted him. "I'd like to hear some of your music."

"Well, it's just too bad I didn't know you had a set of drums, or I would have brought my guitar. You don't have a guitar, do you?"

"No, I'm afraid not. I could never play a guitar. I remember trying when I was little and getting blisters all over my fingers, and giving up. Of course, I'd get blisters from my drum sticks if I didn't wear gloves."

"No kidding?" George sat, sipping his soda thoughtfully. "Well, look here, Alison, I say we ought to jam sometime."

"No! You're—you're not serious, are you?"

"Yeah, I'm perfectly serious. You and me, and I've got a friend who's been playing the bass for years and he can't read music and you can't read music and I can just barely read music. We'd be perfect together!"

"Yeah, perfectly awful."

"No, no! I've got a dream!" he quoted dramatically. "I can just see it!" George's voice was rising, his hand clenching around his glass. "Look, Alison, there's a whole lot of reasons why I want to get a band started. Just look at the world around you. Look at all those people out there who care only for themselves and would walk right over me to get what they want. Look at how miserable they're making themselves in the process, chasing after more and more, until they don't know how much more they could want or even what they want! Inventing misery when they don't think they've achieved enough, just to give themselves something they can feel significant about! All those people, just think if there was something new and different for them to pay attention to, something that would make them think for a change. Just something that they could think about! It's like, mankind is this hugely immature beast that is so emotionally dependent that, once his brain runs out of ways to satisfy itself, all its energies channel into self-destruction! That's why I think the world needs a statement, a statement that it's going to take a few decent people like you and me to get up the gumption to deliver, a statement through music, pure, one of a kind, positive music!" George's face was getting red and he was gasping for breath, but his enthusiasm seemed to be building like an atomic chain reaction, and I stared,

listening to him with bated breath, not exactly swept away on the current of his blather, but transfixed by his raw fervor. "Hey, really, my friend Otis can play the bass like a madman, and he feels the same way that I do! Even if he doesn't know what he's doing—". George's passionate state fizzled into a look of serious reflection.

"Otis? You know a bass player named Otis?

"Yeah, Otis Shifflett. He and I started playing together, years ago, in a group called the Danger Brothers. We split up and he went away to college, but before he left we made a vow that one day we would shock the world. Well, he just graduated this week, and he's moving back to Northern Virginia!"

"Otis Shifflett." I shook my head. "Otis Shifflett returns to Northern Virginia."

"Hey, Otis is probably the best friend I have left in the world. Otis is—he's a font for divine inspiration. Not many people know this, but Otis isn't just a bass player. Otis Shifflett is—the New Messiah."

"Oh, God, now I have to meet him."

"Just think about it, Alison. Do you want to spend your life playing along to radio stations, or do you want a chance to make some real music?"

"Oh, George, really." I sighed. "I don't know. I don't even know why I drum. I mean, I like it, sometimes I even love it, but the whole idea of organizing a band and, you know? Getting together, gee, learning songs, rehearsing, I just don't know if I'm ready, you know?"

"Listen to you. You're putting the cart before the horse. The point is, me and Otis can come over and bring our stuff and we can just jam. Don't worry about having to learn songs, all you got to do is keep a beat, like Otis does. Believe me, the only one who needs to know any songs is me!"

"It sounds like we'd only be doing your songs."

"Well, whose else's? Do you have any songs you want to do?" "Oh, my God, what are you talking about? This is crazy. You're not serious, are you?"

"Of course I'm serious. I've never been more serious. How can I get people to listen to what I have to say if I don't get a group together?" For all his talk about being serious, George really looked sheerly-maniacally-frenzied again.

"But why? What would we be doing it all for? Do you really think there's a single rational reason for three people like us to try to—to do whatever you've got in mind?"

"Rational reason? Putting the cart before the horse." he shot back. "What?"

"Looking for a rational reason to perform music is putting the cart before the horse. If you're half the musician I think you are I don't have to tell you that."

He had only finished half of his last statement before the rest of his words seemed to spring as much from my own heart as his. I sat back, twiddling my soda between my hands, and felt a sensation that was both familiar and excitingly strange, emanating from both of us like some kind of unmistakable trust; it was as if George and I had known each other all our lives. That's what was familiar about it— from that moment on I knew I'd discovered a bond with George, as close as if he were my brother. What was excitingly strange about it was his idiosyncratic alienation, his trademark, that telepathic signal he was eternally broadcasting, saying "Leave me alone", "I know you really hate me", and "So what?", all at once. To try to put this into words is way too complex, I know; in reality, matter of fact, the feeling resulted from exactly the opposite process, I mean, our relationship had broken that kind of barrier, so that everything that had seemed complex and unspeakable had been atomized into meaningless, forgotten pieces of the past. And it was then that I began to know what he wanted, and know that it was the same thing I'd really wanted, ever since I first bought my drum set; to make real music.

"Let me ask you something, George. Do you have any songs that you could play in someone's apartment that wouldn't sound so far from harmonious that the neighbors would call the cops?"

"Look, Alison, I wrote a song years ago that I recorded all by myself in my bathroom, just me and a cassette recorder and my guitar. It's called "The Kitty Song". It goes like this." With that, George began to sing, in a strangely Arabian-esque melody, words that reminded me of something a snake charmer might play:

Well, I left the one that I love,
That's why I'm not smiling…
Yeah, but fortunately,
I don't remember her name…
So I'm gonna go, go, go, go,
Go right out that front door,
Gonna see her no more,
And that's okay with me…

Kitty, kitty, kitty, ee-ee-ee-ee,
You're a bad kitty cat
When you make that me—owwww,
Kitty, kitty, kitty, ee-ee-ee-ee,
You're something at that
Using kitty power, to obtain your kitty chow!

"And then the break comes in, bow, ba ba ba bow bow bow, bow, ba bow bow bow bow bow, Bow, bow bow bow bow bow bow, bow bow bow bow Beeowww…" George was grinning, and conducting with his fingers, as he did this. I was laughing, nodding for him to go on.

Heeeere come kitty, kitty, kitty,
Kitty brainwaves!
Kitty brainwaves control me,
I crave what kitty cra-aves!
Make me go to kitchen cupboard,
What do I see?
Makes me take out catnip pie,
And serve it up to kit-teeeee…

"—And then the chorus is almost the same as before, except this time the cat's using kitty power to fulfill her kitty chore."

"Absolutely poignant." I commented.

"Then it goes—whang, wa wang, wah wang wang, bop, bop bop bop bop bop bop bop, you know, lead break, guitar hero style." He paused a moment to see if I was paying close attention, then waved the air with his hands as if to clear the air of his thoughts. "Never mind, the last refrain goes,

Now my kitty's got me tied up in a padded cell!
Kitty litter everywhere, I smell a kitty smell!
Gonna get her, gonna fix her, gonna make her pay
Gonna have her put to sleep at
The A. S. P. C. A.… .

Kitty, kitty, kitty, ee-ee-ee-ee,
Well, it was nice knowing you,
But who will love me now?
Got no girl, no kitty, I-I-I-I,
I think that I'm gonna cry,
No more kitty power, no more kitty,
No more kitty power, ohhhhhhhhuuuuuuuhhhhhh…

"Aw, that's so sad…" I teased him, but with much admiration for his clever song.

"I know." he nodded, his head drooping toward his chest. "Okay."

"Okay?"

"Yeah, let's do it. Let's record your song."

"Wow, just like that, you decide you want to do it?"

"Yeah, why not. You're right. In fact, if you're half the musician I think you are, we'll be sensational!"

"Yeah! We'll Shock The World!!!! he shouted, almost jumping off the couch. "Just think of it, Alison, the world hasn't seen a legendary three-man power group since Cream! And we'll be even better-legendary, 'cause our drummer's a girl!"

"Yeah!" I broke up laughing and raised my glass of soda. "To the band!"

"I'll drink to that!" George clinked his glass to join my toast, and then wondered aloud, "So, what are we gonna call it?"

"How about…uhhh…" When I realized I had inadvertently used George's trademark phrase, I chortled a bit. George did too, and shook his head.

"No, no, it's gotta be shocking, exciting, bombastic." "New and improved!"

"Right, you got the idea. But the only fair way to decide on a new name is to get Otis in on it. Put it to a vote. Can I borrow your phone?"

"You're going to call him up? Where does he live?" "In Blacksburg."

"Blacksburg? That's where I went to school!"

"No kiddin'? What'd you study?" George was already reaching for the phone on my end table, not sounding very interested in what I'd majored in.

"Liberal Arts, and what do you think you're doing? Blacksburg is three hundred miles away!"

"Actually, about two hundred and fifty. Don't worry, I'll pay you back."

"Well, okay.", seeing that he had already begun to dial the ten-digit long distance number.

"Great." George cradled the phone against his neck and crossed his arms across his chest. "He ought to be home about now."

"I kind of like 'Danger Brothers'," I ventured.

"Yeah, me too, but I don't know about that with a girl in the band… Hey, Otis! How ya' doin'? Hey, guess what? I found a drummer!

Yeah! And guess what? He's a girl! Yeah, of course she's good. Listen to this!" He looked up from where he was staring and said, "Hey, Alison, play something for Otis, he wants to audition you."

"Over the phone"

"Of course, c'mon, hurry up, we're using up long distance time!" I sighed, picked up my sticks, and sat at my drums. "Otis? You still there? Check this out!" George held the phone receiver up toward my direction, and shrugging my shoulders, I pounded out a simple beat. George nodded encouragingly, motioning with his hand to pick up the tempo, and whispered "C'mon, do something wild!" At this point I had forgotten what an inhibition was, and swiftly built up from the plain beat and back beat into a torrid climax that incorporated every piece of my kit. When I had finished, bash, bash, bashbashbashbashbashing on simultaneous cymbals and toms, George smiled approvingly and returned to his conversation. "So what do you think? Yeah!" He looked up at me, circling his thumb and forefinger, and said, "You're hired!"

"Gee, thanks, Otis!" I called across the room.

"So, anyway, Otis, what are we gonna name the band?" George grew silent, listening intently to the unknown Otis two hundred and fifty miles away. "Uh huh. Yeah. Okay…really?" I began to feel like I wasn't in the same room with George, as Otis had apparently taken over the lead in their conversation. I began to wonder how much time was going by, and suddenly remembered the snowfall outside. I went to the window and looked outside, to see that the storm had, if anything, grown in magnitude, and that there had to be at least a "good" foot of snow on the darkening landscape outside.

"George!" I cried out, "Look!"

"Oh my stars and garters. Hey, Otis, I just noticed that there's some kind of natural disaster going on outside." George seemed more amused than alarmed. "What's it like down there? Really? Uh huh…ha ha ha!" I started pacing back and forth in front of him, my expression imploring him to take the situation a little bit more seriously. "Well, look, Otis, I think Alison wants me to make this short. Yeah, I'll tell her. What? Yeah, you'll like her." He smiled craftily at me. "Take my word for it. Yeah, yeah, okay, see you in a couple of days. Take it easy. Later." Finally, George hung up the phone, and gazing at the continuing inundation outside the window, whistled air out of his mouth. "Gee, Alison, am I going to be able to get out of here tonight?"

"I don't think so, George." Suddenly, the excitement of the snow emergency struck me in full force, as I stared at what had already turned into a panorama of nearly-complete white, under the meager illumination of a few street lamps visible through the twilight outside my window.

"Well…uhhhhhh…"

"Yes, it's alright for you to stay here if you want." I smiled at him, courageous enough now to employ the rapport I'd so quickly developed, the trust that came so close to telepathy. George came up next to me, and for a long time we both watched the silent, dioramic miracle of the storm that was both imprisoning us in the apartment and liberating us from our jobs.

"Otis said he could tell over the phone that you are a World-Shock drummer." George finally said. "He said that as soon as the weather permits, he's driving up and bringing his bass."

"Isn't it beautiful? Everything's disappearing…all the cars…all the yards—all under a big, white blanket…"

"And listening to you play over the phone, Otis said he was struck by Divine Providence and instantly knew the name for our band."

"He did?"

"He said it was the weird tonal quality coming over his receiver that did it. It sounded like one of his effects boxes he likes to play his bass through." George turned from staring out of the window and looked at me with an expression of serendipitous inspiration. "What do you think of Phase?"

"Phase?…Phase! Yeah!" I liked it immediately. "It's new, and improved, and …and powerful…"

"Yeah, and fast and hot and aerodynamic."

"My God! You were right! You weren't kidding about Otis being the New Messiah!"

"I do not kid about he who wears the Sacred Grocery Bag on his head."

CHAPTER EIGHT

I opened my eyes, and my room shimmered into focus, illuminated a gentle white, the white that only a few snowfalls of a winter season can catalyze from a beaconing morning sun. For a few minutes I closed my eyes and snuggled in my bed, letting awareness replace unconsciousness, and thinking, still thinking of the dream I'd been having, a cool, breezy autumn night, a great, bright orange half- moon looming large against the black, as it peered over the horizon; red, yellow, and brown leaves crunching underfoot, as he and I walked, and I remembered my arm brushing now and again against his, how strong and warm it was; and it felt so good, I was so happy on our quiet walk together. I love you…I said. I'll look at you, turn your wonderful face to me in the moonlight…I thought. But he didn't look at me, his face remained silhouetted against the trees moving by…Who are you? I don't know who you are, but I love you…you love me, don't you…I can't see you. Look at me! Why won't you look at me?!

Then I came awake, and the new light reflected from my bedroom wall told me it was morning, time for coffee and shower and deciding what clothes to wear to work.

"…Wha…" I groaned, wait a minute, work…what day is it? I turned over in the sheets to look at my clock radio—Thursday, December 16, 7:05, glowed the green l. e. d. display. Fourth day of the week, tomorrow's Friday, so start getting out of bed, Alison—it took about another minute before my usual wakening grumpiness passed, allowing my brain to seize suddenly on the memory of the night before, the afternoon before:

—George! Now I was really shocked into consciousness. My head shot up off my pillow and I drew a frightened gasp. Oh my God, what did I do with George last night? "Ohhh…ohhh…I whimpered, and then timidly lifted my sheet up to see what state my body was in. A wave of relief washed over me, seeing that my underwear was still there. I rolled over onto my back, taking in the gratitude and reassurance that I had stayed good…and then my brain at last started to recollect all the extraordinary things that had happened the day before; the snowstorm, dinner, burgers and talking with George, learning so much about him, becoming friends…then becoming very good friends…and then…

Oh my God, I joined a rock and roll band with George Kerns and somebody named Otis Shifflett?

At this point in the day my brain really wasn't prepared to make sense out of the exciting aftertaste of that yesterday, the exuberant joy that had filled me ever since George and I broke the barrier between us. After all, three years of waking up every morning at the same time to devote the entire day to the same things, isn't exactly going to develop one's mindset toward auditioning for a rock and roll band by drumming over the living room phone, much less whatever that was supposed to accomplish. However, I knew at last that I had, indeed, not taken leave of my sanity when I remembered that, wonder of wonders, No Work Today! I heaved a gigantic, luxurious sigh, stretched and yawned happily in the warm, delicious cocoon of my sheets, and let myself sink back into the sweet embrace of innocent, worriless slumber.

So it was that when I woke up again around nine o'clock I thought little of the fact that there was a man sleeping on my living room couch. I got up and pulled a curtain aside to gaze onto the brilliant carpet of white, yes, no doubt about work being cancelled, which probably meant a four-day weekend. I felt so ticklishly ecstatic to have all this time to do as I wanted, and get paid for it to boot, that immediately I wanted to get all dressed up extra nicely, as I hadn't in so many months, and see the look on George's face when he saw what Alison Riley could do if she wanted.

One shower, one cashmere sweater, one blue skirt with matching stockings, and a few touches of make-up later, I went into the kitchen past the dozing person on my couch and prepared a pot of coffee. I got some raisin muffins out of the freezer and set them on the counter to thaw. Returning to the living room, I turned on the radio, sat in my high-backed wicker chair, and waited for the strains of my favorite classic rock station to revive George.

His peculiar brown eyes fluttered open to the sounds of a cover version of "A Whiter Shade of Pale." He groaned, passed his right hand over his face and through his disheveled hair, and blinked against the unfamiliar intensity of the winter morning light. Then he saw me, smiling and waiting for him, and he propped himself onto his elbows and gawked in appreciation of an Alison he'd never known before.

"Wow! You look great! What's the occasion?"

"No Work Today!" I replied jubilantly. "And the first day of Phase." "Phase?…Oh, yeah…wow." His head fell back against the arm of my sofa and he grinned wackily. "I smell coffee." "Would you like some?"

"Oh, yeah! Wow, this is great. How did you know I liked to wake up to coffee and a beautiful girl?"

"Just a lucky guess. Besides, I figured if we're going to start working together, we'll need to get off on the right foot. Who knows when we'll get as much free time as we have now." I got up and headed for the kitchen to get a couple of mugs of coffee. "Do you take cream and sugar?"

"Not usually, but on special winter mornings, yes, thank you." Still dressed in his work clothes, he sat up and folded his blanket and laid it on the couch beside him. "Sorry if I don't smell too good." he apologized, embarrassedly drooping his head and surveying his raw state of personal hygiene.

I giggled and said, "I don't mind, George, but after you finish your coffee why don't you use my shower?"

"Can't I wear my clothes in there? That's about how much I stink." "No, give them to me and I'll wash them. I need to do a load of laundry myself."

"George looked doubtfully at me, and it was obvious that so many amenities extended was a strange experience for him. He lifted his coffee cup to his mouth with both hands, and I noticed by their slight tremble that he was having a hard time knowing how to accept what I was happy to offer him. Finally, a heartfelt "Thank you." escaped his lips, and I smiled back, "No problem."

The next hour was spent doing laundry while he showered, and when we were finished, the George that sat blinking back at me on my couch looked as refreshed and rejuvenated as I would have expected any twenty-eight year old man to look, at 10:30 in the morning, which was a dramatic improvement over the distraught office services assistant I had found in the supply room the day before.

"Well, Alison, we know that Otis isn't going to be here for a couple of days, but in the meantime we can start working on "The Kitty Song".

"How can we do that?"

"I can go to my house and get my guitar." "And bring it here?"

"Yeah, sure."

"That seems like an awful far walk."

"Hey, don't worry, it'll only take me about an hour."

"Through all this snow? It seems like an awful lot of trouble, for something like that."

"Trouble? It'll be fun. Don't you like playing in the snow?"

"God, George, it's been so long. I mean, I'm twenty-five years old now, I don't think I've really played in the snow since I was sixteen."

"You mean all this time I had so much respect for you, you've been suffering from recreational deprivation? Unbelievable." he shook his head. "Well, look, let me go get my guitar and we can try jamming when I get back."

"Wait, George. Let me go with you."

"Uhhh…no, you ought to just wait for me, this won't take long." "But playing outside sounds like a good idea, George. You're right.

I have been leading a deprived existence."

"Uhhh…but it'll take longer…it won't take an hour if just I go."

"But we've got all day. We could talk about the band on the way. And I don't want to stay here all by myself." It was annoyingly apparent that George didn't want me to come.

"Uhhh…but you're all dressed up and—"

"George, come on, I'd like to see where you live anyway. C'mon, you owe me a favor for doing your clothes." Against this, I knew George would have no defense. Grudgingly, he shrugged his shoulders.

"Okay, suit yourself."

Trudging through a foot of snow was more exercise than I'd had in years. As we stumbled through the drifts and snowbanks, our feet miring and unmiring themselves, George kept muttering about how I should have stayed home and waited, but thoughout my exertion I insisted on opposing his every objection with rationales, the best of which was that the hike would be the start of my program of building stamina necessary for Shock The World drumming. After a while, George stopped grumbling and protesting, but when I tried to tease him into smiling with snowballs he grew angrily silent. That almost made me decide to turn around and go home, but we had already walked more than half the way to his house, so I just shut up and walked in the deep prints he was tromping through the snow.

"Well, here we are." he finally said, with a quick, penguin-like flap of his arms.

We stood before a small, one-story house that should have been white, but thanks to much neglect had deteriorated to a flaking state of appalling squalor. It stood on little more than a quarter-acre of property, as I could tell by the crude wire-mesh fencing, half-buried in snowbanks, that separated the house from the row of similarly ruinous and humble dwellings on its dead-end street. No question remained as to why George was so reluctant to bring me here.

"Gosh." I said quietly after what I realized was a silence he had been dreading, but, by this point, had been reconciled to receive.

"Yeah, I know. Don't say I dragged you out here to see this." "Well, it's certainly different."

He drew a heavy breath, turned to me, and, with a rueful grimace, sighed, "Guess what? This is where it gets worse."

We walked up to the house's porch, once painted what was now an ugly scarring of blue-grey, sagging underneath an A-frame canopy, and with large areas where its slatted floorboards were either missing or, ominously, ragged holes yawned, as if someone had fallen through them. I immediately dismissed the thought of stamping the snow off my boots, and gingerly followed George's tread to the front door. It, too, seemed to be held in place by some miraculous combination of inertia and rust, with a level of security somewhat below that of "I'll huff and I'll puff and I'll blow your door down." Nevertheless, George produced a key from his pocket, and opened the door conventionally; and, having no discrete way of changing my mind and reversing direction, the goosebumps that rose on my flesh as I stepped into the vestibule were the most clammy and indelible memory of the horrible moment when George introduced me to his home.

"In case you're wondering, if I could do something about the fact that this looks like the Black Hole of Calcutta, I would have long ago. It just so happens that I share this house with four people, and this whole downstairs is their own personal urban refusal project." All about us in the claustrophobia-inducing cell that should have been a living room was a dizzying, three-dimensional madras collage of what looked like someone had used a steam shovel to scoop out one month's contents of a dumpster and deposited it therein. This decor effect was enhanced by the liberal appearances of holes that gaped in the plaster walls and an aromatic blend of foot and decaying organic waste odor.

"Four people live on this one floor?"

"Yep. That couch is Fred's. Jeff and Arlene live in one bedroom down the hall, and Franklin lives in the other bedroom. The five of us share the delightful bathroom that won't be highlighted on this tour."

"But where do you—do you…?"

"Where's my room? Voila, Alison." With his right hand, he indicated a grimy panel in the ceiling above the hall. With the same hand he pulled the piece of cord that hung from the panel's edge, and down it swung, revealing a fold-up ladder which George extended to the floor with the haste born of wanting to get this over with quickly and badly.

"You live in the attic?"

"I don't call it living. It's more like a sabbatical from composting." He started to clamber up the squeaking slats of the ladder. "I suggest that you follow me, strangely enough it's really better up here than down there." I made a hasty obedience of his suggestion, thinking that I had never gotten such a view of somebody's posterior upon entering their bedroom.

Compared to the rest of the house below, though, George's attic spread out and welcomed you with a wall-to-wall yellow carpet and a simple decor that actually looked like it had been cleaned within the decade, although the paucity of furnishings could be inventoried within the time it takes to say, "It's been real, and it's been poverty, and a matter of fact it's been real poverty.": carpet, chest of drawers, a crate that served as a table, a closet rod strung up between rafters that kept shirts and pants suspended above the floor, a space heater that was the only apparent source of the barest minimum of comfort, and a guitar case leaning against bare studs; which, along with old, unpainted two by six boards, made up the "walls", whose abbreviated height meant that standing straight was somewhat of an acrobatic proposition.

George sat down, spreading his arms over the back of the couch, and hung his head sadly as he stared into the shallow corner of the attic room. "We're in luck, my roommates are all gone now. Otherwise you could enjoy the frosting on the cake, when Jeff starts complaining about Arlene's cooking and she starts throwing dishes in the sink and yelling at the dog and Franklin comes in with a big bag of Cheez Puffs and a six-pack of Coca-Cola, plants himself in front of the T. V. and consumes four hours of situation comedies and junk food while croaking "Yum Yum!" I've got an extra mattress that I put over the hatch to keep the noise down. Too bad it keeps the heat out, too." he added, reaching down to switch on the space heater. I sat down next to him to get some of the musty hot air that started to blow into the room.

"Why, George? Why do you live here? You must make enough money to afford a decent place to live."

"I've just been unlucky, I guess." he said, still staring into the corner. "It's another long story." When I remained silent, waiting for him to continue, he heaved a sigh and shook his head. "It goes back to when I broke up with my girlfriend. I had to move out of the house I'd lived at with her, and my car picked that time for its electrical system to burn out. It would have cost about twice what my car was worth to fix it, so that essentially totaled it. Besides, it reminded me of—of her too much, so I had it towed away. No car, soon I had no job either, couldn't concentrate on my work. It wasn't long before everything I saw that I had known for so long with her was reminding me of her, too—too much to carry on. So, I decided that I needed a change of scenery, and gave a guy I knew a hundred bucks to move all my stuff to Blacksburg, to live near my friend Otis."

"Blacksburg? But there's hardly any jobs out there."

"Quite right. That's what I learned, after I found a cheap place to live. I was able to get a job for about twenty hours a week at about three dollars and fifty cents an hour. That didn't last very long." George smiled and shook his head again. "Blacksburg was a real cleaning-out experience for me, that's for sure. Otis was terrific. I don't know what I would have done if he wasn't there to talk to. I talked to him for hours about losing my girlfriend, and he offered everything that a friend could to help pull me out of my tailspin. He inspired me a lot, I guess. He's such a simple guy, I remember hanging around his house, sitting on his front porch, spilling my guts out for hours about breaking up with her, and of all the people in the world, he would always listen and give me consolation and strength. If we weren't talking about my problems, we'd go walking along the train tracks or out to the quarry to fish off the rocks. He was like a rock. He was so quiet. He wouldn't say much, but when he did, it was always something like, "Look, George, if there's a girl that you really love and can't live without, there's only one thing you can do about it. Build yourself a bazooka, go to her house, fire a smoke bomb through her window and watch her come running out."

I broke up, laughing, and George's eyes showed a moment of sparkle; then grew sad again.

"But at three fifty an hour and not even working full time, I went broke real fast. I lasted in Blacksburg about three months before I was so sick of living on the edge of starvation, it was enough to make me realize that the benefits of leaving Northern Virginia weren't worth living off of lentils and tortilla chips in the Blue Ridge mountains. It took all the last of my money to rent a truck and drive all my stuff back here. And the only place I could afford—" he spread his arms out in front of him demonstratively—"was the penthouse suite you're enjoying now."

"Well, George, this place is certainly different. But for heaven's sake, how long are you going to keep living like this?"

George's eyes bolted open. For a second, I thought he was going to shout at me, but then his voice came out, coldly and determinedly, as if it was suddenly extremely difficult for him to keep in control.

"Not much longer, I hope. I've been able to save some money by living so cheaply—no car, no utility bills—but that means I don't have a car to move with, even if there was another place that I could both afford, and could get back and forth to work from. So it looks like I'm stuck here for awhile. But I've got plans. I've got enough money to buy this amplifier I've had my eyes on for months." His voice started rising with emotion, and I prepared myself for another one of his "I have a dream!" speeches. "But you know what?" He straightened up, leaning forward and clasping his hands between his knees. "The way things are right now, the way I feel about Joan, makes everything else seem completely unimportant. Right now I could care less if I live in a garbage dump. The only thing that makes sense to me is to get this band together, get—get my songs out, and then maybe— only that way is there a chance that she'll listen."

Seeing from the expression on my face that I was about to raise another protest against the idea of hanging on to such a hopeless dream, George cut me off. "Look, Alison, I don't care what you think about my personal reasons for doing things. The only thing that matters is if those are the same things you want to do. What I feel for somebody is my own business, and I've got the right to feel what I want. That's how I feel, and it isn't going to change." He pushed himself up from the couch and grabbed his guitar case. "We don't need to hang around here any longer, do we?"

"No." I got up, turned off the space heater, and followed George down his attic stairs. I wanted to say more, much more, but the "charm" of George's abode was such that a hasty retreat had never seemed more appealing. In fact, I remember thinking that if I had a choice, I would never go back there again. Once we had left the house, and George had locked the door behind us, I felt immeasurably better, and looked forward with every step to being back in my nice, warm, clean apartment.

We made our difficult way back through the underlying snow in silence, George no doubt brooding on his dreams of escaping the dreariness of his home and putting together a band that would support those wild, pathos-laden dreams of his. I found myself absorbed in my own perplexing train of thought; for a long time, as we walked, I couldn't help but think that there was some kind of paradox, hiding somewhere in all that had transpired in the past twenty-four hours, something that my brain couldn't quite identify, couldn't quite sift out from all the crazy new things that had happened and promised to happen, but it was there nonetheless, I knew it was, and it made me cranky, being unable to put my finger on it.

The question was forgotten, however, when we arrived at my apartment, George set his guitar case in the corner of my living room, opened it, and produced a black, solid-body electric guitar. Without an amplifier, he certainly didn't make an obnoxious level of noise as he played "The Kitty Song" for me, illustrating the melody, harmonies and the tempos that he had in mind. His guitar playing was a foil for his abstracted, eccentric personality; definitely crude, aggressive and slightly spastic, though not so much as his drum style had been. As I listened I tried to imagine how, if I were to jam along, I could complement the ragged edges of his dissonant chords with my own undeniably tighter, more polished drumming technique.

For a few hours, we talked and exchanged ideas, and by the time it was mid-day we were both thoroughly tired of proposing arrangements and alternating rhythms and intros and lead breaks and drum solos, and in fact "The Kitty Song" was beginning to get on my nerves. At about three o'clock I made the suggestion that I might like to take a little nap; and George, similarly, had had enough of Phase work, saying he wanted to go shopping for amplifiers. I watched him shamble off down the sidewalk, and as I lay down on my sofa I wondered for perhaps three minutes why I couldn't identify the strange paradox that occurred to me on the walk from George's house; I was wondering if I ever would, as I basked in the sunlight streaming upon me, falling into a deep sleep.

CHAPTER NINE

"Bri-i-innng!"

I was startled to consciousness by the harsh ringing of the telephone, little more than a foot from my head on the end table. Annoyed from my deep, dreamless slumber, I ignored it for three rings before deciding that there was no use in trying to sleep anymore, and grappled the receiver clumsily from the hook.

"Hello?"

"Hi, Alison, it's me, George. You sound like I woke you up." "You did." I stated flatly.

"I'm sorry. I didn't think you'd be still asleep. It's almost seven o'clock."

"Really?" I rolled over, noticing that I was on my couch and that the living room was unexpectedly dark. "That's interesting." I commented dully, for want of knowing anything else to say.

"Gee, look, I'm sorry, I'll let you go back to sleep."

"No, that's okay. I'm awake now. I shouldn't be sleeping this much in the afternoon anyway." I straightened up into a sitting position, and immediately felt a tension in my neck, that was either from sleeping in an uncomfortable position or crankiness from having my privacy so jarringly invaded.

"Well, I just wanted to let you know that I bought an amplifier." "No kidding? That's nice."

"You don't sound very enthused."

"No, I am, George, that's just great. I just—I'm too tired right now, you know?"

"Oh. Well, wait till you see it. It's got more than a hundred watts of power, and a cabinet that's almost as tall as you are, and built in reverb and inputs for four instruments and everything."

"Great, great." I yawned. "How did you get my phone number?"

"Out of the phone book. I'm calling from a phone booth outside the music store. Actually, the reason I'm calling is because I thought I could save a trip if I brought the amp over to your apartment, instead of lugging it back to my house and then having to lug it back there again later."

I heaved a sigh as my brain wrestled with its first, very definitely unwelcome, decision of the night. If getting a telephone call in the middle of the night hadn't been enough, having to decide if I wanted the start of what, for all I knew, would turn into a parade of amplifiers taking up residence in my nice, clean, and sane apartment, was more than aggravating. Were it not for the fact that I sympathized with George's problems so much, I might have hung up immediately after ordering him never to call me up for such a cockamamie reason again. But too much had come about between us by this point to turn quite so cruel, and I heaved another sign as I forced myself to let him down in the gentlest way possible.

"Look, George, I'm happy you've got an amplifier so quickly, and I'm looking forward to jamming with you sometime, but this is all a little sudden for me, you know? I think we've got lots of time before we have to start doing all these things. I know it may be a big hassle for you to make two trips, but I think I'd rather not deal with any more band stuff today."

There was a pause in the sound coming over the receiver, and mentally I could hear George's brain going, "Uhhh…" Finally, he replied in a subdued, apologetic tone. "Yeah, sure, Alison. Like I said, I didn't mean to bother you. I'll just take the amp home, it's no big deal. By the way, I heard on the radio that the Federal Government's back on schedule to work tomorrow, so I guess the holiday's over."

"Swell." The image of my postponed dictation project barged rudely back to the forefront of my priorities, and I became crankily aware of the tension in my neck threatening to become a full-fledged headache. "Well, George, I guess I'll be seeing you at work tomorrow then." To be sure he didn't think I was brushing him off, I added as cheeringly as I could, "Be careful bringing your amplifier home."

"I will. Well, take it easy. Thanks for putting me up last night and everything. So long now."

"Bye." I hung up the phone and sat back, at a loss to explain the nagging feelings of doubt and anxiety gnawing at my stomach; the lingering suspicion that something had happened, of which I was fully aware but somehow unable to fathom, like some random, disjointed pieces of evidence that separately mean very little but together would drag me toward a contradiction of all the impressions I'd accumulated in the past two days. After about five minutes of contemplation that only made me more conscious of the loneliness of my dark apartment, I felt the strong urge to check myself out in the bathroom, the insecure feeling that came from confronting a problem I couldn't solve.

I walked through the familiar, quiet hallway to my bathroom, flicked on the light, and surveyed myself in the mirror. There were vestiges of the make-up I had put on that morning, some of it smeared in smudges of black from my eyes and red from my mouth. My nice blue dress was also wrinkled from sleeping on the couch. I turned on the faucet and spent a few minutes cleaning my face, until my bare and clean reflection no longer made me feel like I'd been recently victimized. Then I unzipped my dress, removed it and my stockings, put them into my laundry hamper, and looked at myself again in the mirror. For a long, leisurely space of time, my blue reflected eyes studied the brown-haired Alison trembling nearly naked in the glass, perusing how all the parts of my body came together to form what I was. I laid my right hand on my shoulder and slid it slowly along the round contours of my muscles, my bones, my skin, my hair, all that I was on the outside; all that had become so alien to how I felt on the inside. My hand rested in the hollow between my breasts, tasting the warmth and the moisture and the beating of my heart, all centralizing there; and my eyes moved to their own reflection, blinking, blue, searching, and wondering... was I happy? How much of me was still a young girl...? What had twenty-five years done to me...? All these questions remained drifting through my mind as I turned off the light and returned to the living room. I switched on the radio, turned it to a classic Motown station, set the volume down to a low soothing level, and laid belly down on the couch, my head resting on my folded arms. As the music softly filled the room, I let the imagery of the songs transport me to their little, idealized worlds of emotion, and soon, I was feeling better. There's nothing more therapeutic for a confused state of mind than the simple, earnest songs of the Supremes, Marvin Gaye, the Temptations and all the other groups the Motown station played. With their melodies so youthful and enthusiastic and optimistic, compared to the cynical, harsh noises you hear coming out on the modern rock and roll stations. Together with feeling better, I felt grateful of the fact that tomorrow I was going to work again, and everything would be just like I'd come to accept it and it had accepted me.

My mind seemed to clear of its insecurity and loneliness and started to focus on what was obviously the source of all its perplexion—the abrupt change in character that George had brought about in me over a matter of a few wintry hours. I had let him convince me to abandon the basic working philosophy of my ninety- nine percent personality, for a carefree day of indulging everything that was feckless and irresponsible and ultimately insignificant in me, everything that I thought would remain in its proper, hidden perspective forever. And as a result, here I was, alone in my apartment, wearing nothing but a bit of underwear, yearningly examining myself in the bathroom, lying in the dark on my couch, questioning why I was feeling so unsure about something that I couldn't even put my finger on. Unavoidably, as an old Brook Benton song, "Rainy Night in Georgia", rumbled lowly from out of my speakers, I had to ask myself: was I falling in love with George? As bizarrely unthinkable as a romantic reaction to the eccentric office services assistant who lived in an attic might be, wouldn't that explain all this unusual behavior, the dreams I'd been having, my newfound, pensive…vulnerability?

Vulnerability; a quality that I hadn't allowed into myself since the days when I was a college student; a state of being that had been absent from my life for so long I'd forgotten how frightening, how dangerous…how exciting it could be.

I was suddenly aware that I was becoming uncomfortably warm, and rolled over onto my back, the palm of my left hand moving to lie against my dampening brow, my right hand smoothing off the tickling wetness from my thighs. The familiar lushness of "You're All I Need

To Get By" enveloped me as I pondered the fact that I was indeed approaching a state of emotional distraction; incredible as it might be, could it be that it was George I was thinking of, George who had brought on all this exploration of my rising sensitivity, to feelings I knew were born of want and longing and all that had no practical value in the real world? If so, if it were true that my feelings for him were more than mere platonic friendship, why was I so insecure about them?

The answer, I realized suddenly, was no; it wasn't George I was in such an adolescent funk over. The powerful empathy I felt for him had allowed me to know him completely, and even intimately, but knowing him, I also knew that I didn't—want him. No; George was a person who amused me, a guy for whom I might be given to feeling the ultimate limits of sympathy, but these were ordinary and understandable reactions, things I could explain, not the Pandora's Box that stood unopened in my brain, tantalizing me, daring me to crack it open and unleash the secrets I was either unable or unwilling to know. It had to be something that I didn't understand, but nonetheless fascinated and intrigued me, spurring me on, with its mystery, to break the barrier, to know the unnamable truth behind the illusions that, it seems to taunt, were all the knowledges I had.

Phase.

Out of my swirling recollections of the events and contradictions of the past two days, the single word stood out boldly in my consciousness, separate and somehow above the context of scrutability…

Phase.

The idea had so many interpretations, so many connotations, a single syllable that could be a noun or a verb, but just as easily be a description of time or place. It could be a characteristic period of someone's life, something someone might "go through", with a beginning and an end. It could be as innocuous and picturesque an idea as the phases of the moon—like the half-moon hanging in the cool autumn sky of my dream the night before.

Phase; we were going to base a musical enterprise on a term that I had inspired into the mind of a stranger two hundred and fifty miles away, and somehow I would soon meet that strange "New Messiah", and together with George attempt to make it mean—something.

"All you have to do is keep the beat." George had said.

All I would have to do is supply the background, the basis for George and Otis, and Phase would come about. It was simple enough. Too simple, I decided, for it to be the major conundrum that was insidiously boggling my mind. Something as vague and pernicious as that simple word, which after all was merely the synthesis of the theme for a rock and roll band; a word both clever and multi-faceted by intention; was still too understandable to be the cause of the passionate curiosity plaguing me as I lay alone in my introspection.

Inordinately analytical as it may sound, through process of elimination I arrived at the realization that I had succeeded in identifying a recurring trait in the nature of my search for the name of the paradox; in wondering and pondering the significance, first of my feelings for George, and secondly of the word Phase, the common dismissing factor was the answer to the question: why? That is, once I had established the reason why I didn't want George, and the reason why the word Phase, for all its interesting aspects, was really more than just a catchy name, these possibilities had been revealed as implausible to explain what didn't make sense. I had learned quite a lot about deductive reasoning through my experience at the law firm, and through the instinct I'd acquired from years of information retrieval, there was no way I could overlook the pattern, the recurrence of one, key question:

Why?

It was a motive I was looking for.

"Phew." I breathed exasperatedly, the strain of all this intellectualizing having taken its toll on me. I made a mental note of what had taken so much diligence to conclude, and contented myself that at least part of the question, perhaps the most difficult part, had been answered. While the Motown radio station program continued to seduce me into a state of drowsy satisfaction, I finally drifted into a relatively normal slumber, and the last thing on my mind that night was the comforting assurance that the next day would be as wonderfully normal and predictable as a high-pressure administrative assistant position should be.

CHAPTER TEN

Other than the snow remaining in drifts up to six inches on the sidewalks and yards, the next day was just like any other Friday had been for months. Almost everybody showed up for work at the firm, chattering happily about how they had spent their surprise day off and how they were looking forward to the Christmas Party, now exactly one week away. After the unusual way that I had spent my own day off, it did much to relieve any apprehension about the wisdom of starting up a rock and roll band on the basis of George's fancies to return to my good old familiar desk, with the box of supplies all ready to replenish my station, my first project of the day. It also felt good to launch into the dictation project, now that the atmosphere at the office was post-celebratory and I could devote my full concentration to it. It even felt good to see stinky old Joan strut her derriere past me, flinging her purse onto her desk and withdrawing her compact to check her make-up, her usual way of opening for business. Thankfully, the entire day passed just as normally, until around four o'clock, when my telephone rang.

"Mr. Carruthers' office." "Hi, Alison, this is George."

"Hi." I didn't want to reply with his name, as Joan was within earshot. I casually picked up a pen and pretended to be taking a normal business call by doodling an imaginary message on a note pad.

"I just wanted to get in touch with you real briefly. I talked to Otis on the phone last night, and he says if the weather stays like it has for the past couple of days, he can come up to Northern Virginia this weekend."

"Uh huh." I answered in my best business tone.

"He's going to stay in my attic with me until he can find a place to live. How do you like that, now we're gonna have six people using one bathroom at my place."

"That sounds fine." There was a pause in the sound on the other end of the phone, and I smiled to myself to wonder when George would realize that I was executing a cover-up. "Well, anyway, that means we can start working on stuff any time you feel like it."

"Uh huh."

"Is Joan listening? Is that why you're talking so funny?" "Yes, that's correct."

"Okay, okay." George laughed. "Now, look, me and Otis spent a lot of time talking over the best way to get this project off the ground. We figure that maybe the most efficient way to make all our efforts practical is for me and Otis to work together alone for awhile on "The Kitty Song", until he and I have got the chord changes straight, and down to a science. Then, all we'll have to do is get together with you, you'll supply the percussion, and we'll be ready to lay it all down in one or two takes. How's that sound?

"I—uh—think that'll work." I turned to see if Joan was paying any attention, but she was absorbed in entering revisions from a packet of papers into her computer.

"Now, here's Otis's idea. What he thinks we ought to do, once he and I and you have got the whole song perfect, is we should all chip together and rent ourselves some studio time and record it there."

"Hmmm." I thought. Studio time? I had no idea what a recording studio would be like, or how much it would cost, but the immediate beauty of avoiding making high volumes of noise in my apartment sounded very appealing. "What kind of cost are we talking here?"

"Well, it depends on what kind of studio we go to, but we could probably rent an eight or sixteen track studio for about two hundred dollars an hour, which we could split up amongst ourselves. The trick is to have everything you need to be practiced and rehearsed and solid in your head before you go in, so you can, ideally, just go in,

blow off a couple of takes, and split, which saves having to do retakes and overdubs and mixing and that's where all the cost is."

"I see. That would mean about seventy dollars apiece?"

"Yeah, I would guess about that much, tops. It depends on whether they charge you for the tape and how much and what kind of tape you use and stuff like that. So how does that all sound to you?"

"Well, I guess that sounds fine."

"Yeah, once we got a good master tape of our song we can easily make cassette copies, which we can either try to sell ourselves or take around to clubs and bars or even radio stations for a demo tape. That'll work much better than anything we could do at home on our own."

"I agree."

"Swell! Wow, look, Alison, I really appreciate all the things you've done, and I realize I've been kind of a pain and everything, so I just want you to know that I'm not going to make this any bigger a deal for you than it has to be. I mean, when I told you that all I wanted from you was for you to be our drummer, I meant that. I mean, we're not going to be bothering you every night to get together for practice. All I want—uhhh—that is, what I mean is, for now I'd be really grateful if you could, like, set some time aside next weekend so that me and Otis can come over and we can do some rehearsing."

"Next weekend? Let's see, that would be the Christmas weekend?" "Well, yeah, like maybe Sunday?"

"Hmmm…I do believe that sounds like it's going to work."

"Wow, great, Alison! Well, look, I'm gonna let you go, and I won't be bothering you with phone calls or anything anymore. I know you're real busy and frankly so am I. But in the meantime Otis and I are gonna work on The Kitty Song and maybe some other songs, and I'm going to check out recording studios and prices and things. That ought to keep me busy for a week. So, look, uhhh…I'll give you a call—or better yet, are you going to the Christmas Party next Friday?"

"Yes, I am."

"Well, why don't we just plan on getting together then, and I can tell you what I've come up with."

"Very good, sir."

"Very good, sir," he sarcastically imitated my voice. "You're one in a million, Alison. Thanks a lot. Take it easy."

"Yes, sir. I thank you. Goodbye." I hung up the phone and looked again at Joan, not being able to avoid the fear that she had overheard. I could just hear her indignant face and hear her vindicated laughter, if she learned that I of all people was now getting "involved" with a co-worker. She was in the the epitome of her own business-like behavior, however; if anything, she seemed more deeply involved with the task of interpreting the multi-colored revision instructions before her than I'd ever seen her, so many times, attack an assignment like a one-woman school of piranhas.

The following days went by much as if nothing had happened out of the ordinary. I spent much of my weekend shopping for gifts for my family, whom I planned to visit on Christmas, which fell on the following Saturday. I had been able to save up close to a thousand dollars in my savings account, and consequently was able to be pretty liberal about prices. It still took me almost all of the best part of Saturday to find things that suited my mom and dad and brother, and most of my shopping day was unpleasantly spent having to force my way through crowds or waiting in some kind of line. I tried to work up a little Christmas spirit, and went so far as to buy a wreath for my apartment door and cards for some people I know, but by and large I was having a pretty blue Christmas. I remember thinking that it would be a lot different if I had, at least, a boyfriend; how we could get away from all the pushing and shoving in shopping malls that Christmas in Northern Virginia was, year by year, ever devolving into, and drive away in his car to the Virginia countryside where the small, quiet towns were, and we would stroll about the gift shops and antique stores, that were so peaceful, I'd feel sad and lonely with all the beautiful, hand-made treasures if he weren't there with me. I guess you could say that all my Christmas shopping went by in this way, either determinedly searching for gifts that said as much as possible to my family, or daydreaming in some waiting line about a much more serene holiday with an Elvis Presley look-alike. Sunday went by pretty normally, too, a lot of wrapping presents and doing laundry, a little grocery shopping, and letter-writing while listening to Christmas carols on the radio. The most enjoyable part of the day was making a little pile of Christmas cards for all the people who were special to me, including about twenty of my co-workers like Mr. Carruthers and Mr. Gibbs and George. When I was finished, and all my clothes were neatly ironed and hung up or folded in drawers and all my correspondence rubber-banded on my desk, I had some soup and sandwiches for dinner, and then quietly practiced my drumming to the holiday music every radio station was featuring. Though it had been a relatively long time since I'd had the inclination to try to improve my technique, the unique qualities of Christmas music presented an especially interesting variety of challenges for me to provide percussive accompaniment to, lessening the demand for speed and volume and emphasizing wrist and pedal finesse. It was educational and relaxing, boosting my confidence for my anticipated jams with Phase, and my mind centered on trying to make my drumming appropriate for a recording. When I thought to look at my clock radio, I realized that I had devoted two and a half hours to practicing, and went to bed feeling peaceful and satisfied that I had gotten a lot done.

The next week at work was more than usually exciting with preparations for the office party becoming of greater visibility and priority with each passing day. Office service was setting up our board room with tables and decorations, and our receptionist area had an easel with a large posterboard display advertising the event and informing employees that they were allowed to bring one guest apiece for the evening getting underway at four o'clock, Christmas Eve. Other than that, there wasn't an area in the offices that wasn't festooned with wreaths and pine-cone facsimiles of Christmas Trees and shiny balls and even little strings of blinking lights, and though the weather outside was dark and gloomy with clouds, once inside our building the atmosphere was lively and carefree and, really, so beautiful for all the little touches of cheer everywhere you looked.

On Wednesday afternoon I got another phone call from George. He told me that Otis had gotten into town Monday and was staying in his attic, and that they were hard at work on "The Kitty Song" and deciding what other songs to do. He also told me that Otis had gotten part-time work for Christmas through an employment agency and was devoting his free time to looking for an apartment that they could both move into; and meanwhile they were tracking down good, but inexpensive, recording studios. He asked if I was still "up" for rehearsal on the twenty-sixth, and I said he'd better believe it, which produced a whoop from my phone that Joan would have heard if she weren't down the hall at the copying machine. I wished George luck, especially in finding another place to live, and told him I was really looking forward to meeting Otis, to which he replied some joke I didn't quite understand about Otis feeling the same way and baking a cake for the occasion on top of his engine block.

Finally, Friday afternoon arrived, after a day of very little work getting done, and very many preliminaries to the party. Mr. Carruthers had spent the entire morning outside celebrating with his friends at various taverns, and consequently I attended to polishing up a few nearly-completed projects, and when they were done and I had straightened up my desk and sat twiddling my thumbs for a few minutes, I went to the law library to read the newspaper and chat pleasantly with the librarian. After a morning of all this unusually relaxing kind of work, I went outside for my lunch hour and window- shopped a lot, even though I didn't need to buy anything, and I looked forward to my busy plans for the weekend: my brother picking me up, seeing mom and dad in peaceful Pennsylvania, coming back Sunday to meet with Otis and George, and of course, the long- awaited party that afternoon.

By the time four o'clock rolled around, the workstations next to mine had grown increasingly empty and quiet, while down the hall from me, the sounds of clinking glasses and laughter grew from the direction of the board room. Joan was still sitting next to me, tapping away at her keyboard, when I looked at the clock and said, "It's closing time, Joan. I'm going to the party. Are you coming?"

"Just as soon as I finish these documents." she replied, not looking away from her papers.

"Great." I replied, in as light-hearted a manner as possible; it was Christmas, after all. "Let's have an egg nog together, okay?" She nodded yes, and I picked up my purse and headed for the board room.

The room was filled to near-capacity with many of the familiar faces I recognized from work, plus many women and men I didn't recognize who had come as guests. In the corner, behind the teeming multitude of blazer and dress-clad bodies, a tinseled and bulbed Christmas tree flashed and glittered, and next to it on a pedestal stage, Santa Claus entertained the children of the firm's employees and their guests. I made my way to the bar constructed out of tables and covered with white, red and green tablecloths, where I found George Kerns and several other office services personnel serving drinks and snacks.

George was unloading egg nog mugs from a stack of boxes when I walked up to him.

"Merry Christmas, George!" I shouted over the din of the crowd. "Merry Christmas, Alison!" he returned, with a great smile on his face. He was dressed up especially sharply for the occasion, with a gold blazer and matching suit of clothes. "Can I get you a nice egg nog?"

"Yes, please, thank you." He dipped a clear plastic ladle into a crystal punch bowl and poured out a mugful of the rich yellow cream for me. I took it and lifted it in a toast to him. "To Phase." I declared with a giggle.

"May she shock the world." he replied. "Alison, everything is going pretty well with me and Otis. We haven't found an apartment yet, but we managed to decide upon a recording studio."

"Really? Where is it?"

"It's called "Relativity Recording", and it's just outside Richardson on Sycamore Street. It's run by this guy named David Redding that Otis has talked to a lot. Otis said this guy's got a degree in nuclear physics and works at the N. A. S. A. installation in Maryland, and kind of as a sideline he runs this eight-track studio in his basement."

"Gee, a nuclear physicist? I wonder what kind of music a guy like that likes."

"You've got me. Otis said he saw this guy's advertisement on the window of a music store, and, listen to this, the ad said something like 'The expanding universe of your career need not be a mere theory. Contract with Relativity Recording and make your dreams go nova'. Pretty spacey, huh?"

"Yeah, right, I get it. I bet this place would be just right for a group called Phase."

"Exactly. Otis said this guy's into astrophysics and plays music himself, and what's more he only charges a hundred dollars an hour. So, uhhh, anyway, what we've got to do is work all the bugs out of "The Kitty Song" and one more song, and then we can go over there and knock out a two-song demo cassette."

"I'm game. What other song are we going to do? Everly Beverly?" "No, that's way too complicated for a quick, knock-it-out B-Side. Otis and I have been tossing ideas back and forth, we can talk about them

Sunday." He turned and barked, "Yes, sir!" to a gentleman holding up his scotch glass to be refilled.

"Well, I really think we ought to do more normal music, you know?" "Normal? Like what?" he asked, surprisedly. "Egg nog, Mrs. Daniels?"

"Well, you know, something that isn't all weird and silly like "The Kitty Song". Something people like to listen to, like a love song."

"The Kitty Song" is a love song." he retorted, stacking a bunch of tumblers in a neat row.

"Well, yes, I know it is, sort of, but c'mon, George, it's about a guy who loves his cat then gets his heart broken when the cat leaves him and then he threatens to put the cat to sleep and padded cells and kitty litter. I'm not saying it isn't funny, but it does kind of hint at bestiality, wouldn't you say?"

"Well, I admit it isn't exactly the love theme from Romeo and Juliet, but it's supposed to be symbolic, like analogous for love and heartbreak and, you know, real life." He put a handful of used glasses into another sectioned crate.

"That's fine, George, but I think we ought to do something nice and pretty and—you know, happy, to kind of balance out the weirdness."

"That sounds like a good idea." George was looking at me straight on, but with the expression on his face, I felt as if the distance between us might as well be miles. "The problem is, I don't know if I can come up with a nice, pretty, happy song." He bit off my adjectives with a bitterness I found distressingly alarming. I blinked back at him, not expecting such a sarcastic reaction to a suggestion I had made out of completely good and honest intentions.

I didn't think about it at the time, but just then I had become quite annoyed at George's chronic cynicism. To me, it seemed, if anything, a song about sincere, sincere love should be the most natural thing for a real musician to come up with. I knew that George was going through a "phase" of his own over Joan, and for all his claims to the contrary, the shell-shock of a writer somewhat uninspired; but if he couldn't find the means to rise above his failures, especially after all I'd gone through to provide sympathy and help, he suddenly didn't seem like the kind of person I wanted to even associate with, much less record songs about heartbreak over animals.

Instead of continuing to press the issue, I gave the matter a few moments of reflection, and then decided I wasn't in the mood to continue a conversation with him. He had his hands full taking care of all the thirsty party-goers, anyway; so I shrugged my shoulders, put on a sincere-looking smile, and said, "So, George, I shouldn't distract you from your bartending. I think I'm going to mingle in a bit with the party for a while. Why don't you give me a call on Sunday afternoon and we can talk about it more then?"

"Yeah, okay. Take it easy." I left his little bartending scene behind me and strolled into a group of lawyers, who were heatedly discussing the Washington Redskins' prospects and eager to hear my opinions on the subject.

For all the hoopla presaging the event of the party, it was characteristically short and sweet, for after all it was Christmas Eve and everyone was just as bent on getting home to their families and other parties as they were to get somewhat tanked at their place of business. I stayed around, drinking quite a lot of egg nog in the process of advocating which players I thought should be used against Minnesota and delivering my views on many other subjects, based mainly on the authority I derived from a stomach full of creamy rum. Everyone that knew me well got a big kick out of seeing me get pretty snockered, since I had such a reputation as a goody two-shoes, and I went along with the jokes, sometimes pretending to be a lot more inebriated than I was, for the fun of holding on to guys' shoulders and swaying together to impromptu Christmas caroling, and other things that were comparatively naughty for my standards. I finally left, though, slinging my purse with just a bit of difficulty onto my shoulder, and making some excuse, when the party had dwindled down to about twenty people, and Mark Davidson's (he was one of the Vice Presidents) hand was displaying dissatisfaction with merely fondling my waist, and I was starting to enjoy it a bit too much. So I headed down the hall to my workstation to get my coat.

There, sitting in her seat with her head face down on her desk top, was Joan.

"Joan!" I cried. "Are you all right?"

Her head rose from where it had slumped over her elbows, and she blinked at me through tears that had streaked her face with blue and black rivulets. Her lips were blubbering, her hair fallen in unkempt strands over her hot, reddened face. She was gasping for breath, gulping down her tears, staring directly at me, but seeming almost like she didn't see or recognize me.

"Joan! What happened?"

"You!" she wailed, as if on the edge of insanity. "Alison Riley! How are you today, on this day of days?" she babbled hysterically.

"I'm fine, Joan." I said, drawing near her and laying my hand on her shoulder. "I didn't see you at the party. Aren't you feeling well?"

"Oh!" she cried, and to my shock she had grabbed me around the waist and had buried her head against my stomach, her back heaving in sudden spasms as she sobbed into my dress. "Oh! I'm —f —f—"

"Joan, honey." I tried to comfort her, squatting down so that her head was on a level with mine. "Please don't cry. I can't stand to see you cry."

"Alison." she finally gurgled with a whimper that was like a baby, "I feel so awful—I kn-know you think I-I hate you—but I don't—I look up to you so much…I feel—so awful—so alone—ev—everybody here hates me—!"

"Hates you? What are you saying? You've got to be the most popular person in the firm!"

"No!" she raised her head and shook it at me. "That's how it might look, but all the men in the firm take me for some kind of little toy they can play with, and—and all the girls, th—they hate me because of it!"

"Joan, nobody hates you. I think you're a beautiful, hard-working woman and you've got more brains and guts than anybody I know."

"Tha-thanks, Alison, but I hear what people say about me. And a lot of it's true, I do act like a little boy-toy, it is all my fault. And it's because—Ali, I've got to tell you something."

"Go ahead."

"A—Ali—" she stammered out, "I came from a ve—very poor family. My parents and my brothers and sisters lived in Appalachia. My daddy was a coal miner, or he did what kinds of odd jobs he could get, and sometimes there just weren't any, and I'd see him sitting on the porch just staring at the hills—I hated to see him like that…when I was little there wasn't always enough to eat, and I'd go looking in the woods for berries if there wasn't snow on the ground… my-my sister and I'd have to sleep in the same bed at night. Daddy—he worked— worked so hard, when there was work, a—and he would come home sometimes at night all covered with coal dust, put a single loaf of bread on the table and some eggs in the ice box and th-that would be our breakfast, lunch and dinner for days— sometimes a whole week. All my life, Alison, I dreamed of having enough money to live in a nice house with nice clothes and never be hungry again." She had calmed down enough to sit up straight on her own, and pulled a handkerchief from her purse, to daub at her face.

"Oh, Joan, I had no idea…"

"No! No one does! There's no way to describe what it's like to live on the edge of starvation, especially to someone that's never been through it—the way that nothing, nothing matters, not pride, not love, not anything, when all you want in the world is—is even a little crust of bread…I remember dreaming about big plates of beans…b—b— beans". Her shoulders started to shake as she fought against the tears and ironic laughter her memories were bringing.

"But, Joan. Why are you telling me this now?"

"Be—Because it's Christmas, and here I am, doing fine for myself, and my daddy's still back in the mountains, i—in the cold—I don't know if he's got enough to eat—he'd lie to me and tell me he's doing fine, even if he's hungry—my—my daddy—if he could see the way that I have to behave to get people to like me in the big city here, I think it would break his heart, even if it's all I know how to do. And— right now, I just couldn't bear to go into that party and carry on like I usually do, not with George Kerns in there, not with anybody—I just need to be alone."

"Are you sure that's a good idea? It sounds like you maybe ought to have someone around to talk to."

"Thanks, Alison. I f—feel like a real idiot telling you all this. I just want you to know— the reason I act the way I do—why I had to do what I did to George—is I see a lot of the way I used to be in with him. He would sacrifice a successful career, and live in an attic with a space heater and bare light bulbs and eat beans, just so he could write music and do all the other things he thinks are important, and I just couldn't stand being with a guy like that, even—even if I loved him.

I couldn't stand anybody like that—I—I couldn't stand failure of any kind. I need to keep away from that—it just drives me insane to see anything that looks like the way my—my daddy lives." She sat staring at her hands crossed in her lap, and I took in all the dizzying effect of feeling sympathy, through the buzzing of all my egg nogs, for the last person on earth I would have expected to.

The stultifying experience of finding Joan in tears, and learning the shocking truth of her desperate past, would have boggled my mind even more profoundly if I hadn't also come to an amazing revelation. For, now I knew the name of the paradox that had been defying me for more than a week. I had been staring me in the face all along, but I had been too assured in seeing my own point of view to notice the one thing that hadn't made any sense to me; the motive that I couldn't understand, because of my own, thickheaded conviction that I could understand anything and everything I wanted:

The reason that Joan had gone into George's attic that night almost four weeks ago.

CHAPTER ELEVEN

Thank God Christmas finally came. My older brother James arrived at my doorstep at seven o'clock in the morning, knowing that I never could sleep later than that when I knew there were presents to open. James worked as a computer programmer and consultant for businesses in Pittsburgh, and I always felt eclipsed by him because he could spill out hours of technological terms about post files and readouts and link-ups and computer languages that I hadn't the vaguest conception of, and he knew it and would get this smug little condescending grin on his face and I'd sometimes have to scream and punch at him to make him shut up. Besides the fact that he was some kind of technological genius (if you had any doubts about that, he would tell you) he was by and large a big, happy nerd with no appreciation for anything that was vaguely asymmetrical. He couldn't understand why anybody would pay money to see a movie that wasn't a sequel to Star Wars, Rocky, or Rambo. His musical vocabulary was limited to two songs:

Da da da da, da da, da da da dah, oh yeah!
Da da da da, da da, da da da dah, oh yeah!

was one of them. He wrote it himself, when our family was driving on a two thousand mile car trip, and he never seemed to tire of it, even years later. His other song was a blues number that he wrote himself:

Have you ever been to Pitts-boigh?
Have you ever been to Pitts-boigh?
Have you ever been to Pitts-boigh?
Have you ever been to Pitts-boigh?

**Well if you've never been to Pitts-boigh
Get on the bus and go to Pitts-boigh!**

I guess I loved him a lot because he was my brother, but I can't remember a time when I wasn't glad to see him leave.

It was wonderful to see Mom and Dad, who wanted to know about all my boyfriends. When I told them that my closest male friend was a guy named George who wrote music, they grew kind of quiet and asked if I was working too hard. James did most of the talking, as usual, sipping on beers and expounding on his annoyances with the primitiveness of the computers he had to program, and his customers who had the nerve to try to operate his programs in any way but the way he had prescribed, and as usual, I would withdraw to the kitchen to work on a jigsaw puzzle I'd solved and taken apart countless afternoons before.

Of course, we all had Christmas Dinner and then sat around the living room to open our presents. Good old James got a little computerized music keyboard; that made me mad, especially when he started punching out

Da da da da, da da, da da da dah,

and yelping, "Oh, yeah!" Over, and over, and over. I loved the beautiful clothes Mom and Dad gave me, don't get me wrong, but why on earth did they give James something like that? Didn't they know I had to ride back with him three hundred miles to Virginia?

The best part of Christmas was the evening, when we all sat around the fireplace and talked about Christmases when James and I were little and we'd stay up half of Christmas Eve night eating candy canes and telling ghost stories and waiting to see if we could catch Santa Claus. Mom laid down on the couch and pulled the quilt I had given her over herself, and told her own favorite stories, like the one about how James would always try to frighten the babysitters she would hire for him, by throwing shoes down the stairs after they had put him to bed; and the time I had seen some ducks quacking in the pond next to our house and tried to walk out to play with them, until I had walked, and fallen, in over my head and was lucky that the next door neighbor's son heard the ducks and my splashing and saved me from drowning. Dad threw some stories in himself, like the time he thought James was old enough to baby sit me, and he had left him in charge while he went down the street to visit one of his friends. I remembered nothing of the episode, but Dad said I had started crying and crying and nothing James could do would shut me up, so James took me by the hand and led me down the street to where Dad and his friend were talking in the garage, crying all the more furiously all the way, because James hadn't thought to put any clothes on me.

I went to bed that night in the same bedroom I'd had from when I was thirteen until I had gone away to college. Three hundred miles away from Washington, D. C., in a house with a yard and a porch that you could see the mountains from, it was so quiet and peaceful to snuggle up in bed with a mystery novel, I'd always feel a little sad, because these interludes could never last very long. That Christmas night I turned out my bedside table light and thought about Joan Stevens and her awful past; how it must have felt to have had to fight for mere survival all those years, how the world must have looked so hostile and painful to her as she grew up; how everything had changed when she started to become a beautiful woman, and suddenly she could make everything turn around for her.

Of all the people in her vast circle of acquaintances, it was I to whom she had bared her piteous secret; I, with my own, once precious secret, of which I had been so stupidly proud, and of which I now felt like a petty fool to have held it so important and dear, compared to the trials Joan had gone through.

The next day James and I kissed Mom and Dad goodbye and sure enough, James had programmed his stupid keyboard to go

Da da da da, da da, da da da da, ding-dong!

over and over again. He set it on the dashboard of his Camaro and sang along with it for about fifty miles, until I grabbed it and threatened to throw it out the window if he didn't shut up. He apologized and asked for it back, saying "I'll be good," and when I stupidly believed him and handed it back he turned it on again and locked it in the glove compartment. Like always, I wasn't exactly heartbroken when he dropped me off at my apartment.

I was tired and cranky from the three hundred mile trip, but excited about the jam session scheduled for the afternoon. It was still only about eleven o'clock, so I took a quick shower and changed into my bluejeans and tank top, which are my favorite, most comfortable clothes for drumming. Seeing that it was still quite awhile before I could expect George to call, I laid down on my couch to take an energy-building nap.

This time, when the phone rang beside my head, I was ready for it. "Hello, George." I said.

"Hello yourself. But this isn't George." came back a deep, serious-sounding voice.

"Oh, I'm sorry, I was expecting a call from someone else."

"That's understandable. He's right here. I'm Otis Shifflett, musician."

"Oh!" I laughed. "I've heard so much about you. Is it true, what George told me, about that test you administered to one hundred co-eds at Radford University?"

"Oh, yeah, the double-blind test to determine if girls really brush their teeth. That test was one of my most conclusive research projects. After all, this is a question men have been pondering for time immemorial."

"Ha ha ha!" I laughed. His voice reminded me of Rodney Dangerfield's, it had the same kind of bronchial inflection, but at a deeper pitch.

"Why are you laughing? Are you one of those women who tries to pretend she's brushing her teeth when she goes to the bathroom? Huh?"

"Ha ha ha! You found me out!"

"That is my gift and my curse. It is the way of Otis Shifflett to see behind the way things appear, and know the way they truly are."

"Really? Are you a mind reader, too?"

"Yes I am. For instance, at this very moment I can tell you that I am thinking of a—a Grecian urn!"

"Don't let him fool you, Alison!" George's voice came from the background over the phone. "He's really thinking about how much a Grecian earns."

"I just said I could read minds. I can't be held responsible for typographical errors."

"What a great idea for a song! The "Typographical Error" Blues!"

"You are a typographical error,

Giving me the typographical error blues…"

"By George, George, I thought you said you couldn't write a love song!" I laughed out.

"Yer not an error in grammar,

Giving me the typographical error blues…"

"Uh, look, guys, your song is really pretty, but why don't you two save your enthusiasm and inspirations and come on over?"

"We're on our way."

Fifteen minutes later there was a knock on my door. When I answered it, there was George, accompanied by a guy about his own height, wearing a sheepskin coat, with black, curly hair and a big, hooked nose that hung over an unsmiling but friendly looking mouth. Both had black guitar cases in their hands.

"Hi, Alison. This is Otis." "Pleased to meet you."

"Likewise, ma'am," he replied in a serious voice. "I understand that you also share the aspiration to shock the world."

"Well, I don't see any harm in trying."

"Very well. After this point, I will not be held responsible for any instances of spontaneous combustion or pregnancy. Please note that you are doing this of your own free will and under the auspices of the Geneva Convention. Let's get down to business."

They brought their guitar cases into my living room, and I followed them outside to help them unload their amplifiers from Otis's car. Both amps were almost as tall as I was; George's was sticking out of Otis's trunk, the hood tied down over it with clothesline. Otis's amp completely filled the back seat of his old, green Pontiac. As we struggled to bring them up the stairs, I hoped that none of my neighbors were watching.

Once the amplifiers were set up in my living room, Otis and George produced their guitars from their cases and slung them over their backs.

"You'd better get ready." Otis said to me in an ominous voice.

Suddenly, I felt nervous and woefully inadequate; the moment of truth had arrived, and I hadn't expected how it would feel to actually be called to produce solid, real music, right on the spot. I picked up my drum sticks, again, not foreseeing that my hands would become wet and slippery, and went to sit on my drum throne while George and Otis connected cables from their instruments to their amplifiers. Then, both of them flicked on switches in the backs of their amps, and two low, hissing, wind-like sounds rose up and filled the room.

"Ready to tune up?" Otis asked, still with the air as serious as someone about to fire an atomic weapon.

"Ready." George answered. "Give me an 'A'."

For the next five minutes, as I sat trying to calm my nerves, the two guitarist played notes back and forth to each other. I had never seen a tune-up session, and it bewildered me to see George holding down his strings high up on the neck of his guitar to pluck a note, then twisting the pegs to stretch the strings to produce the same note on another string that he wasn't holding down; and then lightly touching the strings high up on the neck and producing notes that sounded like little chiming bells. I later learned that these were called harmonics.

When they were finally satisfied that their instruments were in tune, Otis turned to me and, without speaking a word, started plucking his bass with his forefinger, generating a steady, fast beat with the even, rhythmical throbbing of a motor:

buddabuddabuddabuddabuddabuddabuddabuddabuddabudd a—

His eyes never departed from mine, and I could tell he was waiting for me to join in. Taking a deep breath, I said a silent prayer, and then he started to add cracks from my snare to his beat:

budda-crack-abudda-crack-abudda-crack-abudda-crack-abudda—

We continued in this way for about a minute, his big, dark eyes hardly ever blinking as he bit his lip in concentration, and I focused my brain on learning and maintaining the tempo. Then, Otis said, "Come on!" and his fingers started to roam all over the neck of his bass, playing intricate, powerful notes, while my beat and his own remained constant. All of a sudden I realized that I had it, I had the beat down, there was no way I was going to lose it, and I started throwing in my own fancy embellishments, rolling from tom tom to floor tom, adding a series of cymbal crashes, all the while never deviating from the snare bursts that defined the original beat.

After Otis and I had jammed with each other for about five minutes, in came George with his guitar intro, and for the first time on earth, Phase performed "The Kitty Song". George shouted the lyrics, to be heard above all the instruments, and when it came time for his lead break, both Otis and I dropped out completely while George screwed his face into a grimace of concentration and executed the notes with all the grace and style of somebody loosening the lug nuts from a truck wheel. When his lead was approaching its finale, I marked out a one-two-three-four

crack-crack-crack-crack

and the three of us "slammed" into the final refrain and chorus. When we had finished, and the final notes of guitar and bass had faded away with the wash from my ride cymbal, I remember thinking, George had been right; we had done the song as close to perfect, the very first time, as anyone could have possibly hoped.

"Well," said Otis. "No need to work on that one any more. Let's take a break." He took off his bass, switched off his amplifier, and leaned his guitar against the grill cloth. George did the same, and we all sat on the couch to talk over the situation.

"To paraphrase Socrates, no man of sense would deny that we've got a hit on our hands." Otis declared somberly.

"Yep, see, what did I tell you, Alison?" George added.

"I would say that you're just about right. This is bigger than all of us put together."

"Well, I'd say that there's no reason we couldn't go straight into Relativity Recording right now and knock that one right out." George continued.

"Yeah, but George, what are we going to use as a B-Side?" I postulated. "There's no sense going in there and turning out just one song, without another song to go with it."

"I'm glad you asked that, Alison." George replied, "Because Otis and I gave that matter the benefit of our intense scrutiny, and we decided that…there's no way in hell that either of us could come up with a love song. But—" he brightened, lifting a finger for emphasis, "We have come up with the next best thing. Shall we show her, Otis?"

"We shall. We should."

They went to their instruments, put them and the amplifiers back on, and George started strumming his guitar and whistling a rather sad, wistful little tune; Otis joined in on bass, and they both swayed gently in time to the haunting, delicate and engaging chords. I myself started nodding my head, lulled into a languid, peaceful state of mind as the tender melodies intertwined in a quiet, sweet expression.

But then, George's strumming pattern converged on a single chord, increasing in speed and intensity, as his hand moved the chord up the neck of his guitar, higher and higher, faster and faster, until he was thrashing his instrument like a barbarian to arrive on one, sustained, almost agonizingly dissonant chord—and then, he and Otis started pounding out one of the most insistent, grinding, plodding series of power chords I'd ever heard, while George brayed:

> The rock of your brain—
> Is lifted away—
> Behold the squirming worms!
> Don't hand me that line—
> That love sermonette—
> You are what you eat—
> Yummy, creamy, worm omelette!
>
> Ev'rybody hates me Ev'rybody hates me
> Ev'rybody hates me Ev'rybody hates me
>
> I know you're against me—
> I know what you think—
> So what's my reaction—?
> Uhhhh…poopy-stink!
>
> Ev'rybody hates me Ev'rybody hates me
> Ev'rybody hates me Ev'rybody hates me

But why do you hate me—
What crime have I done—?
In each waking moment—
Public Exile Number One!

Ev'rybody hates me Ev'rybody hates me
Ev'rybody hates me Ev'rybody hates me

I have the solution—
I hate you right back—
I hate you so hotly—
I have—hate attack!

Ev'rybody hates me Ev'rybody hates me
Ev'rybody hates me Ev'rybody hates me
Ev'rybody hates me Ev'rybody hates me…

When the final chords had faded away, I was left stunned by the brutal fever of George's musical onslaught. That one song had seemed to sum up George's whole personality in four refrains and choruses, all the rejections he had suffered, and his reactionary embrace of the grotesque and dangerous in response, with a heavy, self-parodying theme of infantilism for the sake of dark humor. What could I say? The damn song was George.

"Gee." I offered.

"Well, what do you think, Alison. Is this going to be the next 'I Can't Get No Satisfaction'?"

"It—it's got a good rhythm."

"So, come on, Alison. Try jamming on it with us."

I was reluctant. This travesty of normal human emotions was not exactly my idea of an alternative to a pretty love ballad. Every part of me wanted to be somewhere else, anywhere else—but how could I reject a song like that, at that point, after the way that George had executed it, like it was the most meaningful thing he had ever written? I was more than reluctant—but I picked up my sticks once again, and waited for George to begin that deceptive introduction. When the bass and guitar power chords started to blast into me, I blinked my eyes at the unexpected harshness of this alleged music.

Then, as if to fend off the waves of malevolent force that were relentlessly bombarding my ears, I began to flail at my skins, marking time with the chords, no longer knowing why, or even quite what, I was doing.

CHAPTER TWELVE

Starting with the point after George and Otis had driven off in the Pontiac, the whole world began looking and behaving radically different for me, as far beyond my control as if it were a car that had hit a patch of ice on the road. I wasn't quite myself when I went back to work the next day. To begin with, I had tossed and turned in bed until about two o'clock in the morning, unable to get the thundering chords of "Ev'rybody Hates Me" out of my head. I couldn't decide if I hated that song or was in awe of its unforgettable, rampaging, monolithic structure. In fact, my brain had this ludicrous image of gigantic ogres stomping around and wiggling their butts in some kind of mad syncopation to the rebounding thrusts of George's song. I think I was mostly distraught because I had really wanted to do a simple love song, and instead George had brazenly gone in the completely opposite direction; but there was no way I could deny that "Ev'rybody Hates Me", for all it's ironic lyrical content, was on the surface a funny, catchy collection of licks, and isn't that what's important for a successful commercial song? Who was I to say it wasn't a good song to do? I didn't like it, that's all.

The other thing that bothered me was Joan. After she had unburdened her soul to me the Friday before, we hugged each other a lot, and then she grabbed her coat and stumbled off, ignoring me when I asked if she was alright. With the kind of mind and behavior she exhibited, there was no telling what to expect from her when Monday rolled around. Maybe she wouldn't even come in.

So, due to lack of sleep and with all these misgivings in my brain, I was pretty dazed and confused when I shambled into the office. The first big surprise of my day was seeing Joan sitting at her desk, starting her work before I did. The second big surprise came when she smiled and gave me a little present.

"Here, Alison. I want you to have this."

"Oh, thank you, Joan." I hugged her and opened the little box. There was a small, round locket with a thin gold chain inside. I opened the tiny, golden door of the locket, and inside were engraved the words, "Please be my friend."

"I'm so glad to be working with someone like you. I don't know if I can change, if I can ever be the kind of person you would like, but I want you to know that if there's anything in my power to do it, I'd like us to be friends."

Oh brother. My head was spinning. I thought I had just gotten used to the water, ever since Joan turned into an iceberg a few weeks ago and started diluting our workstation to the temperature of the Arctic Circle. Now she was as chummy as a kitten. This was an awful lot of cutesie-pie to encounter after the kind of night I'd had.

"Joan, I don't know what to say. Of course I'll be your friend. You never have to worry about that."

"Thanks, Ali. I feel so much better now." She sat down and started working again, and I went to my seat and put on the locket.

For my next surprise, George called up that afternoon around four o'clock. "Hi Alison, I've got some good news. I've talked to David Redding, and we've got an appointment at twelve o'clock Saturday to record for an hour. Are you up for it?

"Yes, I guess so."

"Okay. David Redding's got an amplifier at his studio that I can use, and Otis is going to bring his bass amp. You should get your drums packed up so we can load them into Otis' car. Then we'll go into the studio and knock out a couple of songs."

I had a lot of misgivings about leaping into professional recording so soon, but, just as I'd acquiesced to drumming on "Ev'rybody Hates Me", it seemed as if there was no way to resist the momentum of the chain of events. I agreed with George that I would meet with him on Saturday, and thought no more of Phase for the rest of the week.

George and Otis arrived in Otis's station wagon that Saturday. It was a bright, sunny day, and both of them were wearing T-Shirts. I had put on my tank top and bluejeans again. We loaded my drums into the back seat of the car and drove off towards the outskirts of Richardson.

We arrived at a brownstone townhouse that had a set of six concrete steps and a porch with a swinging chair on it. "This is the place, 4314 Sycamore Street." George announced.

We ascended the stoop and walked up to the front door, I with my drum sticks and George and Otis with their guitar cases. There was a little brass plate over the doorbell that read "Relativity Recording". George rang the doorbell and, after a minute, the door swung open.

The man who opened the door stood almost a foot taller than George, the tallest of us. He had bright, straight blond hair, a lean, youthful face, and remarkably light blue eyes that shone behind a pair of wire-rimmed spectacles. A waft of air blew from inside his house as the door stood open, and I detected the scent of cologne and freshly-brewed coffee. He nodded and smiled a big, toothy grin at us and said, "You must be the 'Phase' group. Come in, come in. I'm David Redding."

I don't know quite how to put this into words, but something about his tall, lanky body, that "gosh darn it' grin of his, and those gorgeous blue eyes produced an immediate reaction in me. Suddenly, the palms of my hands had become damp, and I had to wipe them against the legs of my jeans, which had also seemed to become tighter and tinglingly confining as I had to lower my eyes in embarrassment. Looking at his long, lightly haired arms, and the veins that rippled through them, and his long strong fingers, I thought I was going to get dizzy and faint. He was like a god, a tall, blond, nuclear physicist god.

"Can I offer you some coffee?" he said, with a lighthearted, friendly bouncing on his heels. "Off the clock, of course."

"Yes, thanks." George and I said at the same time.

"And you, Mr…?"

"Shifflett. Do you have any milk?"

David led us to his living room where we sat, George and I on a couch, and Otis on a matching recliner. David's decor was simple and tasteful, with a raised area, in front of three bay windows, where there was a globe on a stand and a sophisticated-looking telescope. I sat next to George, clutching my drumsticks in my lap, as excited as a schoolgirl and growing more so by the minute, savoring the exotic, professional ambience that had bathed me from the moment David had opened the door. Up until then, the idea of buying studio time had only registered as a risky seventy-dollar waste inside my brain; now, the investment seemed like the most fantastic bargain I had ever made, anticipation of drumming under the direction of this nuclear/astrophysicist sparking from my deepest nook and cranny to the tips of my fingers.

"Is it my imagination or is it hot in here?" Otis observed.

David Redding returned from the kitchen with a platter of steaming mugs, sugar, cream, spoons, and a tall tumbler of milk. He set it on the coffee table in front of George and me, and sat down in an overstuffed chair next to an oaken writing desk.

"Well, it's good to meet three enterprising young musicians. You all seem like a charming bunch. I've never had a group with a female drummer in my studio, I'm really looking forward to a unique experience." He grinned that overwhelming, make yourself at home grin again, and I came as close to melting as I ever had, two simultaneous trickles dribbling into the cloth of my tank top as I returned his extensions as best I could; a frozen, idiotic smile. "Now, is there a leader or spokesperson for your band?"

"No, we're sort of a democratic conspiracy." Otis replied matter-of-factly. "Alison and I back up George while he executes shameless ruses. Well, maybe some of his ruses are shameful. Are you ever ashamed, George?"

"I think so, but I'm usually too busy failing at something to notice." he quipped. "I guess you might say I'm the leader of the band, Dave. Otis and I have known each other for years, and he and I work out the arrangements for the songs I write. Otis doesn't work from any traditional musical framework; he just picked up the bass one day and kind of locked himself into a room with it, and when he came out…"

"My mind and my instrument were as one. With my mind I crouch behind the bush in the clearing and am not to be seen."

"I see. And you, Alison, how do you fit in with all this?"

"Well, I met George at work, and one day we both got snowed out of work and went to my apartment and I showed him my drum set, and well, uhhh…"

"Alison is a phenomenon. Alison is the rhythm of the planets. Alison is the graphite rods in the Phase nuclear reactor, to couch it in terms you can understand."

"'Phase'…" David replied, his long fingers moving to rest on his thoughtfully pursed lips. "I really like that name. And I like the idea of a girl drummer. What say we go downstairs, and let you all see my studio?"

We walked to a door in the rear of David's kitchen and followed him down a flight of stairs, past a laundry room, to a great heavy door set into a long, cinder-blocked wall, that looked almost like it guarded a bank vault.

"I've done all the carpentry and design for this studio myself. Soundproofing, of course." he explained as he opened the door, and I saw that its nether side was covered with what looked like foam cones. "I know it's not much, but it's plenty for the kind of music I like to record."

The room was about fifteen by thirty feet, with the same foam cones covering most of the walls, cables running over the floors, and a group of amplifiers along the wall to the left as we entered. On the wall to the right was a group of tables, with consoles and tape decks and electrical equipment, where all the cables radiated. There were a group of microphones on stands clustered in the far left corner, with cables leading to the consoles on the tables.

"You should set up your drums in front of the amps," David instructed, "While you and Otis set up in the center of the room." he indicated to George. "I'll get all the microphones set up and we can start a sound check in the meantime."

It took about half an hour to get everything set up the way he told us. A couple of times, while he set up boom mikes in front of my drums, he leaned over close enough that I could smell his scent, and once, while he connected some cables on the floor, he looked up at me with a glint of fire in his eyes, and I made a silent vow that I would play like I had never played before, if not for the sake of our tape, then to express the magical instinctual attraction I felt for David.

Finally, we were ready to go. David sat behind his equipment, counted us down from ten to one, and pointed a finger at me to begin. I started up the song by clacking my sticks together for a four- count

clack-clack-clack-clack

and then the three of us started jamming out "The Kitty Song". I think that Otis and George could feel the magic that was inspiring me, challenging me, enabling me to turn out a percussive display that expressed all my most brazen feminine passions, because they too slammed from one section of the song to another with hairs-breadth accuracy; and, as before, when the final chord wailed and faded away, we knew that it had been a flawless, brilliant take.

Then we did "Ev'rybody Hates Me." For this, I let George and Otis supply all the enthusiasm, for my own part merely adding a rather rote beat/back beat. I put an oblivious expression on my face, hoping that David would be able to tell that I was just along for the ride on this one.

When we had finished, having once again turned out a perfect recording the very first time, David played back the songs for us over his monitor speakers.

"I like them. I don't think I've ever recorded music that came out so well the very first time." he remarked. "I wonder if you all would let me work on the tapes a little bit myself, free of charge?"

"What do you mean by work on them?" George asked.

"Well, I think I could insert a few extra touches on keyboard or guitar that would make these songs just a bit more listenable. That is, only if you'd like them to get engineered a bit."

After a brief discussion, Otis, George and I agreed to let Dave augment the tape, after which he could produce a batch of twenty cassette copies for us at the cost of a dollar apiece.

We packed up our equipment into Otis's car, thanked Dave for helping us, and he waved at us from the porch of his house, saying, "Keep on writing those songs, and I hope you record with me next time."

Otis dropped me and George off at my apartment and left to go to work at his part time job. George sat down on my couch and I went to fix us a couple of sodas.

"That session took a lot out of me." George said. "It's funny, but suddenly I feel so empty—like I've said all that I can say, and there's nothing left to say or do."

"I know what you mean." I replied, sipping my soda. But it feels good. In a way, I'm really glad it's over. Now all we have to do is wait for David to send us our copies of the tape, and we can take them around. The hard part's over."

"Maybe for you it is." George set his drink down gently. "But for me, the hard part has just begun. Now I have to see if Joan will like the song."

Ohhh, nooo…I thought. "What do you mean?"

"I mean I'm going to send her a copy of the tape."

"George, I still don't think that's a good idea. In fact, I think I know it's not a good idea. You must get that girl out of your head."

"And I told you I can't. How can I describe to you the way it is to love a woman like I love her—like I'll always love her? A love that will kill me if I don't do something about it?"

Just like before, I did know, I understood everything he said, even before he had said it. This time, though, the feeling of empathy was more profound than ever, as I though of my own, killing passion for David Redding, passion that I knew would never be realized…

…unless…

I reached over to George and placed my hand over his own. His pained, brown eyes met mine as I gently but firmly took his hand and placed it on my left breast. I slowly closed my eyes at the sensations that welled from his sudden, intimate touch, and leaned back on the couch, letting my mouth open as my heart began to race, pulsing against his hand through the smooth, sheer tank top fabric.

"There is an answer, George." I breathed softly. "I will be your Joan…and you be my David." I opened my eyes to see his astonished expression. "Don't think about it. You think too much already. Please— hold me. Love me. Take me." I pressed his hand down, chafing my soft, thrilled bosom, and gasped as his fingers began to clench, squeezing my flesh, my blood, as it rushed to swell in long, hard tips desperate and demanding his abuse, his adoration, insane, immediate crushing.

His lips came down upon mine, and his strong tongue lunged against my own; sweet, wriggling, rasping, they clashed in our clamping mouths, as he slid his hand up under the bottom of my shirt to ravish my hungering upper torso, then down, following the tiny hairs that led below the edge of my jeans. As his hand delved and cleaved against the supple material outlining my womanhood, my fingers hurried to unbutton his shirt and unfasten his belt, and I tore my mouth free from his to taste of the powerful cords of his neck and the hard muscles of his chest. I felt my jeans snapping open, and blazed into an indescribable state of joy as they came away from my thighs, revealing my satin underwear to his irresistible exploration, playing over my most sensitive contours, drawing gasp after wonderful gasp from my rutting body, tickling, probing, teasing, seizing, and pulling at my waistband and forcing the luscious material against me. I leaned back and moaned and shuddered.

"David! David!"

"Joan…my sweet Joan…" he murmured back.

All the outside world disintegrated from around the glorious frenzy that climbed and climbed and finally exploded, leaving us spent, trembling, and once again, George Kerns and Alison Riley.

EPILOGUE

The next Monday I arrived at my usual time at the office, said "Hello" to Joan and proceeded to set up my desk. The day went on as it had for years, typing and filing and phone calls and spending lunch with Joan, wandering and window shopping. The whole day passed without a word from George.

So did the next day. And the next.

I didn't find out for five days that George had disappeared. I mean completely disappeared. I found out from Derrie Grant, who said that Personnel had been trying to get in touch with him since Monday, and neither his roommates nor his parents could provide a single clue.

Otis called me up one weekend and said that he didn't know what had happened to his friend either. He took over residency in George's attic and said he was going to stay there until George came back.

After another couple of weeks there was another office service services hired to replace George. By the time another couple of weeks had passed, Joan and I stopped whispering to each other with theories about what had happened to George, and as the months went by, the memory of my strange, star-crossed friend became once-again overwhelmed by the normal, day-to-day activities of my working-girl life.

Six months after he'd disappeared, which was last week, the news story came out that a body had been found in the desert of New Mexico. It had been identified as George Wayne Kerns. He had apparently wandered, on foot or by hitchhiking, all the way from Virginia to the middle of the desert, where he had slowly died of starvation and exposure. One item that had been found on his body was a handwritten transcription of the words to Bob Dylan's song, "Simple Twist of Fate."

I still love my drum set. I polish the rims and cymbals and stands, and every once in a while I try to play a song. Joan hasn't married, but she's trying; and I still put on the locket she gave me, almost like a ritual, every day. I wouldn't say that we've become friends, though, because of the secret story in our past that, neither of us can bring ourselves to accept, was written by us.